# THE LAND OF PERCEPTION AND TIME

# THE LAND OF PERCEPTION AND TIME

## A Mystical Journey of Self-Discovery

KEVIN MURPHY

Waterside Productions

Printed in the United States of America

First Printing, 2021

ISBN-13: 978-1-956503-51-7 print edition
ISBN-13: 978-1-956503-52-4 ebook edition

Waterside Productions
2055 Oxford Ave
Cardiff, CA 92007
www.waterside.com

*For my parents, Leo & Terry. Thank you for all the love
… until we meet again.*

# TABLE OF CONTENTS

Chapter 1: Playing in the Field . . . . . . . . . . . . . . . . . . . . . . . . . . . . . . . 1

Chapter 2: The Lottery . . . . . . . . . . . . . . . . . . . . . . . . . . . . . . . . . . . . . 9

Chapter 3: A Time of Innocence . . . . . . . . . . . . . . . . . . . . . . . . . . . . 14

Chapter 4: A Visitor in the Night . . . . . . . . . . . . . . . . . . . . . . . . . . . 25

Chapter 5: "Be Carlos for a Day" . . . . . . . . . . . . . . . . . . . . . . . . . . . . 44

Chapter 6: The Reflection in the Mirror . . . . . . . . . . . . . . . . . . . . . 60

Chapter 7: The Pupil Becomes the Teacher . . . . . . . . . . . . . . . . . . 70

Chapter 8: New Teachers Emerge . . . . . . . . . . . . . . . . . . . . . . . . . . 91

Chapter 9: Just Be Me . . . . . . . . . . . . . . . . . . . . . . . . . . . . . . . . . . . 104

Chapter 10: Doubting Thomas . . . . . . . . . . . . . . . . . . . . . . . . . . . 120

Chapter 11 : Enter Dr. Jon . . . . . . . . . . . . . . . . . . . . . . . . . . . . . . . 127

Chapter 12: Living the Laws . . . . . . . . . . . . . . . . . . . . . . . . . . . . . 151

# CHAPTER 1
# PLAYING IN THE FIELD

*Once upon a time*, there were three friends and they all played together in the *Field of Potential Probabilities*. Playing in this field of energy was not like anything you have ever experienced. They didn't communicate with each other like people you know. They didn't use words to talk to each other. Instead, they communicated with their thoughts and feelings. They were eternal beings.

As soon as they thought about being someplace, they were there. It didn't take any time to travel to get there because they didn't have physical bodies like humans do. They were beings of light. In fact, in the *Field of Potential Probabilities*, or the *Field* as they called it, there is no concept of time. There is only eternity, so their concept of space was different too. In the *Field*, everything happens simultaneously.

Everyone in the *Field* was happy all the time. They only knew how to feel good because they only felt love. Each of them loved to play among the physical stars and planets too. They were fascinated with what took place on all the planets, but they couldn't visit one in physical form unless they were assigned to go there – and when they were assigned to a planet, they couldn't move around like they could in the *Field*. Everything was slower because everything was influenced by perception and time. That's how these planets got their name: the *Lands of Perception and Time*.

The three friends loved to watch the formation of these different physical planets. Their favorite was a place called Gaia, though they didn't quite know why. They were just drawn to it. It was captivating and intriguing. Yes, the exterior was exquisite. That was a given. But it was the vibrations that came from Gaia that was the main attraction for them. They loved to feel the contrast emanating from this particular *Land of Perception and Time.* It projected powerful emotions of both love and fear.

They first noticed it when tiny pieces of cosmic dust and gas started merging together to form a large sphere of glowing red-hot liquid. When the surface cooled down, the liquid became a solid crust. Steam forced its way to the surface and the rains that followed gradually formed vast oceans. Volcanic activity on the ocean floor led to the formation of several land masses on the planet. Then it slowly started to develop tiny life forms: single-cell organisms. Eventually, oxygen was released into the atmosphere and multi-cell organisms started to thrive.

The three friends enjoyed watching the plants and other vegetation grow. But the real fun began when the eternal beings started getting assigned to Gaia. This allowed them to transform into human beings and truly get to experience themselves. When you feel love all the time, the only way to get a true appreciation for it is to feel the *absence* of love. The more you feel this absence, the greater the desire to feel its presence. When eternal beings visited these *Lands of Perception and Time,* this was what they experienced.

Although Gaia was a hard place to get assigned to, the three friends continued to envision going to Gaia together. They understood that they would have to transform from their current energetic forms into physically dense bodies. That was okay with them.

One day they were talking about what it would be like on one of the *Lands of Perception and Time,* which they referred to as the *Lands.* Leo always seemed to be the most curious.

"What if one of us decides to stay on a *Land* and not come back?" he asked.

"That can't happen, silly," responded Terry.

"Why not?"

"Because when your dash ends, you have to come back."

Carlos was listening but he was confused. "What do you mean? What's a dash?"

Since Terry was the only one of the three friends who had previously been assigned to a *Land*, she explained. "When you get to the *Land*, they mark down the day you arrive. They call it your birthday. Everyone who goes to a *Land* always leaves and comes back here. But in the *Land*, when someone leaves the planet, they record the day they leave. Between those two dates is a dash – which signifies the time you spent on the *Land*. While you're there, you don't know how long your dash will last. For some people the dash feels very long, and some people's perception is that their dash is much shorter, but everyone's dash will end. For some reason, humans seem to focus continuously on that ending instead of enjoying the experience of being there. They don't realize that it's all happening right now. That's how they experience the absence of love instead of feeling its presence."

"That doesn't sound like fun," said Leo. "I'm very happy staying right here."

Carlos jumped right in. "Not me. I can't wait to go. I want it more than anything else!"

Leo turned to Carlos and asked, "Why do you want to go so badly?"

"I want to feel what it's like to be me."

"But you can feel yourself now," countered Leo.

"It's not the same," said Carlos. "I want to be able to feel like I feel now, but I also want to experience the absence of love in a human body. That's the only way I will know the difference."

"I can understand that," said Leo before shifting directions. "What else do you want to do while you are there?"

"I'll let my human-self decide most of the things when I get there," Carlos replied. "But I can think of a few right now."

"Such as..."

"Such as running through a field of grass and feeling the gentle breeze on my face ... such as walking along a beach and splashing water high in the air with my feet... such as watching a sunset while feeling the warmth of another human's hand in mine."

Terry nodded her approval. "And of course, you'll want to breathe."

Carlos chuckled as that was not high on his list of things to do on Gaia. "Every human has to breathe. I'm talking about the fun stuff."

"I don't just mean every human's innate intention to live," Terry clarified. "I mean being *aware* that you're breathing."

Carlos glanced over at Leo to see if he was grasping what Terry was trying to say. Leo just shrugged and then looked back at Terry with a confused look.

"Breath is our connection to your human self," Terry explained. "As soon as your breath stops, you come back here. So, you want to keep breathing as long as you can. Most humans are not aware of their breath, and as long as they are not aware of it, they are not aware of their connection to us. So, if you can get your human self to be aware of its breath, it will be more aware of you."

The others mused over this. Then Leo said, "Okay, okay, enough of this talk. Let's go look at Gaia."

They all agreed and then they were instantly observing their favorite planet. It was majestic. On the surface, Carlos didn't know what he loved more: the blend of aqua colors reflecting from each body of water or the red-orange hues of the mountainous terrains. The orbital spin of the *Land* only made it that much more intriguing. This was what brought them joy. They loved to watch the evolution of the planets, which were in a constant state of expansion. They would line up in the clouds with other eternal beings and watch what was taking place on the *Lands*. There were so many vibrations coming from Gaia that the three friends could feel the energy... but not all of it was positive.

"Why can't they feel us?" asked Carlos.

"Low frequency," answered Terry.

"Do they even know we're here?"

"Some of them do … but most of them don't."

"I'm going to change that when I get there," said Carlos emphatically.

"Good luck with that," Terry replied.

It was fun for them to imagine what it would be like to be assigned to a *Land*. They always listened intently to stories from other eternal beings who came back from Gaia. Everyone who returned said that they experienced a tremendous period of growth while they were there, but they would have liked for their human self to maintain a more regular connection to their eternal being.

As they continued to observe Gaia from afar, Leo shared a recent encounter that he had with another eternal being. "Sheldon told me that he just came back from a *Land* with a better apprecia-tion of the *Field*."

"What did he say it was like?" asked Carlos.

"I'll tell you myself," answered Sheldon.

Carlos turned and was startled to see Sheldon right next to him. He looked at Sheldon and asked, "was it everything you hoped it would be?"

"Was it all fun and games?" Sheldon started. "No, it wasn't. My biggest challenge was staying physically healthy. When I was a young man, I fell from the ceiling of a room I was working on and badly damaged my knee. It never fully healed. Later on, I struggled with the debilitating effects of cancer. But even though I suffered from poor health, the love I shared with other humans was remarkable. It always made me forget about my health."

Carlos listened intently. "Would you ever want to go back?"

"Absolutely," Sheldon replied without hesitation.

"But you suffered so much while you were there."

"Yes, that's true. But there were amazing times as well. Now I know that I would focus more of my energy on feeling love in all situations, like we do here in the *Field*, so I could be a greater influ-ence on both my human self and others."

"I don't get it. How do we influence what our human being is doing?" Carlos asked as he kept his focus on Sheldon.

"I didn't do a really good job at it, so I guess you just do your best to be a positive influence on your human self," Sheldon responded.

"I can do better than that," said Carlos. "I'm going to make my presence known. My human self is going to understand what I'm communicating to it."

"That's not always the case, Carlos."

"Well, it will be for me," he said emphatically. "I want to remember who I am and feel what it's like to be me while I'm in a human body."

"How are you planning to do that?" asked Leo.

"I have no idea. But I will constantly try to teach my human self how to feel me."

"I'll give you a little tip," said Terry. "Just keep thinking and feeling love and your human self will have greater potential to maintain that connection."

"Of course, I will," Carlos replied confidently. "And my human self will get to know me. I am sure of that."

"You say that now," countered Terry. "But once your human self begins to mix thoughts with fear, you begin to lose the conscious connection between the two of you."

"Why would my human self ever mix a thought with fear? Why wouldn't I mix everything with love?"

"You get trained to interpret all the physical vibrations from the *Land*. Not all of them are loving, so it's not so easy to remember what it feels like here in the *Field*."

"Well, that is my whole purpose for wanting to go to Gaia," said Carlos. "I want to remember the feeling of love I have right now."

"It'll take patience," said Terry. "Your physical senses will be so busy responding to the impulses of the *Land* because you have to get programmed for survival first. Then you forget about the things you really wanted to do when you got there."

Leo frowned. "We won't remember what we're planning to do before we get there?"

Terry shook her head. "We decide what we want to experience after we get there. Once we're in the *Land*, we vibrationally become who our human self decides to be. Remember, you don't have to be in the Lottery that assigns you to one of the *Lands*. That's your choice. But once you get to the *Land*, who you become is your human self's choice. We just honor it. The free will of your human self is to be you or not to be you. If it chooses not to be you, then you must become it anyway … because you are just a reflection of your human self's free will to be who it wants to be."

Carlos was intrigued. "You're saying that humans are choosing to be love or not to be love … and if they choose the absence of love, that is what they must experience?"

"Exactly," said Terry.

"There seems to be a cruelty about that … doesn't there?"

"It's not a cruelty, it's a contrast," Terry explained. "Part of the beauty of experiencing yourself in human form is all the contrast that you get to experience. You get to pick and choose what you like and dislike. Some of it turns out to be loving and some of it not. But as a human, you develop a greater appreciation of love when you also experience the absence of it."

Terry paused before continuing. "When you come to appreciate that love, the trick is to get your human self to maintain that vibration, or the frequency of love, regardless of what's going on around it. That puts it in alignment with you, and the longer both of you maintain that alignment, the faster your human desires show up in physical form. And just like here in the *Field*, if you maintain that vibration … it must manifest. The only difference is, as eternal beings, we know it must manifest. But as humans, you don't."

"Then I will teach it to my human self," said Carlos confidently.

"That is why you will be there too … so your human self doesn't have to do it alone."

The three friends continued to gaze out at Gaia. Despite its stunning visual effects, it was the energy that was projected out from Gaia that truly captivated their attention. That was the energy that was always reflected back to Gaia from the *Field*. Sure, it wasn't always positive, but there was a remarkable consistency within the expansion of its vibrations. Love was still the most powerful force on Gaia.

The setting was tranquil. As the orange ball of sun slowly dipped behind their view of Gaia, the three friends were in quiet awe of the beauty they were witnessing. Leo broke the silence and asked Carlos, "If your human being is ever able to listen to you, what do you want to tell yourself when you get there?"

"Whatever my human being desires, I am going to become it," said Carlos. "So I guess I would keep saying, 'I am perfect and I am you. Everything is done, it's just waiting for you.'"

"That's a beautiful message," said Leo. "But how do they hear us? I heard they use their ears for hearing by interpreting sound vibrations."

"They may not physically be able to hear us," said Carlos, "but I know they can still feel us when they have heightened emotions. That's why I'm going to give my human being a strong dose of love!"

"That is the best way to establish your connection to your human self," Terry acknowledged. "I hope it feels all that love you will be giving it."

Carlos was ready to find out.

# CHAPTER 2
# THE LOTTERY

As the sun peeked its head above the horizon, brilliant rays danced across the universe with a mammoth tail of orange, red and purple streaks. It was a foreshadow of what was to come. This was the day of the Lottery, when eternal beings would be assigned to different *Lands*. The three friends couldn't conceal their excitement.

Carlos stared at the mélange of glorious colors that lit up the sky. The anticipation of the lottery was filling him with exhilaration.

*Why haven't I ever done this before?* he thought to himself. It didn't matter. He was in the lottery now.

Leo, Carlos and Terry all hoped to go to planet Gaia. Even though they would lose their memory of the *Field* while they were there, they hoped they could all still get to experience it together. There were many different situations they could be placed into on Gaia, but they would always be connected to the energy of the *Field*, and with kindness and love they could continuously try to influence the human beings that they would become.

Other eternal beings joined them and added to their collective feeling of euphoria. They all seemed to come and go very quickly. In actuality, they were all always there since everything happened simultaneously in the *Field*. They just learned to focus on one thing at a time, which lent the appearance of things happening sequentially. Only in the *Lands of Perception and Time* did they truly feel the illusion of separation. This was an illusion they were ready to experience.

The three friends gathered together in a small circle as the Lottery was about to begin. Regardless of where they were assigned, they knew they would all meet back in the *Field* to share their experiences with each other. They didn't know what circumstances they would be born into, but they were excited to manifest into human beings.

Terry looked at Leo and then back to Carlos and said, "No matter what happens, we will always be the Three Amigos!"

They all cheered in unison, "To the Three Amigos!"

As they were preparing for the numbers to be assigned to the eternal beings, the three friends looked out across the landscape and saw the multitude of beings gathered around. Carlos could feel the overwhelming emotion of love. He was intoxicated with delight. The eternal beings who were watching from the distance were all the ones who had not signed up for the lottery yet. They were not ready to take the plunge but they were all there to support each other. Every one of them knew that the greater frequency of love they all generated as a collective consciousness would ultimately help those who were assigned to the *Lands.*

Carlos surveyed the scene and took it all in. There seemed to be billions upon billions of illuminated souls stretching out for as far as he could see. There was no end in sight and the expansion of the gathering led to greater feelings of joy and elation for everyone involved. Carlos wondered where they were all coming from. He had never been aware of so many eternal beings. The collective consciousness of the gathering was one of excitement, compassion and love. A feeling of gratitude overwhelmed him. In that moment, he had an unmistakable knowing that he would be selected to visit one of the *Lands.*

Slowly the numbers were drawn. As each eternal being was designated to a specific *Land,* all of the eternal beings enveloped them in what would best be described as a group hug. It was a wonderful moment for all of them because they were all connected within the *Field,* and could all feel the designee's powerful emotion of gratitude.

The three friends waited anxiously for the next number to be announced. The number 112428 was burst across the sky with the same orange, red and purple streaks as they witnessed earlier. Carlos looked excitedly at his number. It did not match. But his disappointment was quickly transformed to excitement as he turned to Leo.

"Yes!" was Leo's initial reaction when he became the first of the Three Amigos to be selected. As they glanced back up to the sky, they saw the designation of the *Land of Perception and Time* for Leo. It said:

112428 – GAIA – Ayreland.

Much to his delight, Leo was assigned to go to Gaia, and was to be born into a family in a place called Ayreland. Leo moved forward so he could be acknowledged by all the other eternal beings. Carlos felt the overwhelming emotion of love pour forth. He could only imagine how it felt for Leo.

Carlos stayed close to Terry while more numbers were called. They had always hoped to be close to each other on one of the *Lands*. As new instructions were flashed across the sky, Terry shouted, "That's me!"

525627 – TRITON – Flatland

Terry was being assigned to the *Land of Perception and Time* called Triton. Although she wanted to be near her friends, the excitement of being able to explore Triton filled her with joy. The love and gratitude she felt was amplified by all the eternal beings who joined with her to celebrate.

Carlos was ecstatic for his friends and he continued to wait patiently as number after number was called. He kept sending positive energy to each soul being assigned. He was always the most adventurous of the three friends and could never stop talking about getting assigned to a *Land*. He was also the most excited to go but his assignment was becoming less certain.

He started to feel the irony of his friends getting assigned when maybe he wouldn't get picked at this lottery. He quickly shifted his focus to picturing himself as a human being on Gaia and feeling love in his human body. While he held onto that feeling, the next instructions were delivered:

205708 – GAIA – Adelphia

"That's my number!" he exclaimed. He checked again to make sure it was correct. A feeling of gratitude and bliss enveloped him. It was a vibration that reverberated not just through him but throughout the *Field*. This was a greater form of love than he had ever felt before.

*Why wouldn't it be?* he thought to himself. It was being magnified across the whole Field. He was grateful for all the eternal beings who had showed up to share in his joy. And now he would be going to Gaia at the same time Leo would be there. He held onto the feeling of love and appreciation he was experiencing in that moment.

When the Lottery was completed, Carlos gathered with his friends. Leo was trying to contain his enthusiasm as he began to speak with a calm and cool demeanor. "So...we all got selected. How about that?"

Terry nodded in agreement. "We certainly did."

Carlos was still a little too emotional to respond right away. After collecting himself, he finally shared his feelings. "I'm so excited to go, but I can't believe I am not going to be able to remember either of you while I'm there. That is going to be so strange."

Leo was already thinking the same thing. "I know. We won't be able to communicate with each other...and we may not even be able to communicate with our human selves."

"Don't worry, Leo. You won't miss being in communication with us while you're in the *Land*," said Terry reassuringly. "Nor will you feel any frustration if you are unable to communicate with your human self. I don't know how else to describe it. You'll just always be there guiding your human self along."

Carlos was ready for his new human experience. He felt a strong vibration of love in that moment as he turned to his friends. "I'm ready to go, but is it okay to tell both of you that I will miss you?"

"I will miss you too," said Terry.

Leo agreed. Then he looked at his friends and said, "See you back here."

The three friends proceeded to the designated entry point for their particular *land*. There were rows and rows of doors that stretched out for as far as they could see. Each door accessed a portal that would transport the eternal being into a specific time and place in the *Land of Perception and Time* to which they were assigned. They gave one last wave to all the other eternal beings who were there to send them off. They each stepped through their own door and into the portal that would take them into another dimension. Throngs of eternal beings – spread out across the horizon – watched intently as the lottery group slowly disappeared through the doors.

# CHAPTER 3
# A TIME OF INNOCENCE

Upon the birth of his human form, Carlos tried to adapt to his surroundings. His thoughts couldn't instantly produce results like they could in the *Field*. Being in a physical body was not like anything he had ever experienced before. He could feel every cell in his new body. They all condensed into a conglomeration of energy that delighted his senses. In some ways, it felt as though he was still in the *Field*. But in other ways, he knew he was experiencing a different dimension because of the density he felt as a human. Still, the love he felt inside his body was undeniable. It was the same love he felt in the *Field*.

Looking through the eyes of his human self, everything felt so lucid yet he was seeing things for the first time. He was an eternal being and a human being in this body together and they functioned as one unit. They could each feel everything that the other part of them felt. The feeling of love and appreciation that Carlos felt inside was overwhelming.

His birth parents called him Kenny and Carlos loved being called by his new name. He felt like he was bursting at the seams with love and delight as he, in his new baby form, kicked his arms and legs in all different directions. Other human beings picked him up and constantly hugged him. He could feel the energy of love pouring through them. He wondered where all the contrast was. Everything was wonderful, just like in the *Field*, even though it was physically exhausting. He loved all the new sensations he was experiencing, but he also valued the time that they called sleep. That was when he was no longer confined to the trappings of his body.

Every morning, the sensation of light peeking through the beige shades of his bedroom window would start a miraculous process that seemed to kick-start his physical body. He would become more alert and he could sense Kenny's full attention shifting to the external stimuli all around him. Whether it was the melodic sound of his parents' voices, the warm smiles they continuously gave him, or simply the feel of his soft clothes massaging his skin, Kenny was enthralled with it all and absorbed everything he could. He kept constantly processing all the information that bombarded him through his physical senses. He was like a computer program installing all the information into its hard drive.

In the late afternoon, whenever the opportunity arose, Carlos would look through Kenny's eyes past the sliver of open curtains and watch the last flashes of sunlight shine into Kenny's room. It reminded him of sharing the celestial rotation of the sun with his friends back in the *Field*. Kenny, his human self, didn't remember those moments but he sure seemed to enjoy the sunsets he was witnessing here on Gaia.

After all the stimulation throughout the day, Carlos found that the process of falling asleep at night was one of his favorite experiences. As he lay in bed, there were levels of awareness that he went through that would bring him closer and closer to his eternal form. Once Kenny reached the point of a deep sleep, that was when Carlos could temporarily expand his consciousness beyond his human body. He was no longer bound by the limitations of Gaia. Carlos was free to move through the dimensions of space without having to deal with the influence of time.

That was when he would find himself zipping across the *Field* without the confines of the physical apparatus that they called his body. Although his energetic connection to his human form never ceased, the freedom was exhilarating. It wasn't that he didn't enjoy being in his physical body. He had just expected to be able to have more interaction with Kenny while in his human form. He wanted to share what he knew with him. He wanted to tell Kenny why he'd wanted to join with him in the *Land of Perception and Time*. That was not happening, as Kenny was transfixed on taking in everything from his physical environment. He was in a constant state of sensory overload. Carlos hoped to change that.

Over the first five to six years of his life, Kenny just kept absorbing everything he could translate through his physical senses. During those early years, there was little interaction with other humans beyond his two parents and close family friends. Fortunately, he didn't need other friends in order to play with the deluxe train set his father had built for him in their basement. Aside from the four different types of trains and the twelve feet of tracks, there was a small village with tiny plastic figurines of people mulling about. Each morning, these toy figurines would come to life in Kenny's imagination. He gave each of them names and they would play in the park while waiting for the next train to arrive. After loading the plastic figurines on the train, Kenny would watch them make imaginary stops all across the country. Carlos was delighted to see Kenny so happy. It was just like being back in the *Field*. As soon as Kenny thought of a place where he wanted his train to go, he was there.

Kenny also experienced the love and affection that his parents continued to shower upon him. He had a perpetual smile that was only enhanced by the freckles dotting the landscape of his cheeks. His stark blue eyes were in direct conflict with the mop of red hair that accompanied the freckles. Kenny was a joy to behold when around his parents yet he was still comfortable with himself when he was alone. He was in alignment with Carlos and didn't even know it.

Unfortunately, this happy phase in his life didn't last too long. Eventually he started to meet more children and he came to realize that not everyone was sending out positive vibrations. At home, he would enjoy spontaneous bursts of laughter with his parents. Playing with other children, the laughter was often directed at him, not with him.

Each passing year, it became more apparent that Kenny didn't have the physical stature that many of his classmates possessed and valued. During his elementary school years, he became the target of much ridicule and jokes.

"You can't run fast at all!"

"You stink at basketball."

"Kenny's a little weakling."

"You're no good."

Once he started middle school, it felt even more strange for Carlos. As Kenny interacted with the other school children, he developed feelings that were not consistent with Carlos's emotion of love. These were things that Carlos had never felt before in the *Field*...and they didn't feel right. They included shame and blame and guilt. As Carlos tried to turn up the volume of his positive vibrations, there seemed to be a disconnect that was taking over. Kenny was mirroring other children's emotions and they weren't always pleasant. This phenomenon would continue throughout his school years.

Kenny couldn't understand why so many of the other students were ridiculing him. To make matters worse, he kept processing all the information they would throw at him. Carlos was conflicted. Initially he was excited to experience all the joys and disappointments that Kenny went through. But as the years passed, Kenny kept storing away more and more of the negative energy he received from other children. Carlos tried to help, but Kenny was not listening. He spent more of his time at home and less with other children. Home became a quiet sanctuary that made him feel welcome and safe...but even that didn't last.

It already felt lonely at school and now it started to feel lonely at home too. Most of the boys he knew had siblings they could play with, but Kenny was an only child. The other boys would usually tell him how much they hated their siblings, but he knew they didn't really mean it. They had permanent companionship with someone at home. It was something that he lacked.

Kenny wasn't aware that he was complaining about this whenever he got the chance. The same could not be said for others. Sam sat next to him in 8th grade science class and was one of the few students who talked to Kenny on a regular basis. His long blonde hair was constantly covering his eyes, resembling the appearance of an English sheepdog. He also bore the brunt of Kenny's frustration.

"What do you think my parents are waiting for?" he asked Sam during a break in class. "Why is it taking them so long to have another kid?" He wasn't really expecting an answer to the question.

Sam shrugged. "Maybe they can't have more children."

"Why wouldn't they be able to have more kids?"

"I heard my mom talking about it one day," said Sam as he flipped his hair back from his eyes. "Apparently, moms can't just have kids whenever they want."

"Well, I know my mom is going to have another child," Kenny said confidently.

"It's not always so great having a sibling," Sam countered. "My brother drives me crazy. Why would you want a brother anyway?"

"I don't want a brother," Kenny responded defensively. There was a slight pause as he thought about what he'd just said. He wasn't going to be talked out of a sibling just yet, so he quickly added, "I really want a little sister more than anything." A big smile came across his face at the thought of having a younger sister.

⚜   ⚜   ⚜

Barbara Haneg never expected to have only one child. She could always identify with the story of little Orphan Annie, primarily due to her own bright orange hair, and the fact that she also didn't have any biological siblings. After she gave birth to Kenny, her small frame took a while to recover from the delivery but that still didn't rule out having more children. Her husband Matthew was the driving force behind that decision. Matt Haneg, with his tall frame and his jet-black hair, was an avid fisherman and hunter. After working fifty hours per week as a labor negotiator, he spent most of his weekends on their twenty-one-foot Grady White. He would have preferred a larger fishing boat, but this was what they could afford. During the winter months, hunting trips would replace fishing and fill up his weekends. He purchased the fishing boat and the small cabin for hunting because he always envisioned sharing this time with his family. When it became clear that Kenny was not interested in either fishing or hunting, his father chose to continue these hobbies for himself. His mother objected at first, but then she began to enjoy the greater amount of free time she was able to spend with Kenny – especially with him at home so much.

By the time he was a young teen, Carlos was amazed at how instinctually Kenny was able to protect his body. He developed a keen awareness of balance and he was able to sense potential danger before it came. It was a great learning experience for both of them. The ability that Kenny possessed to sense danger was starting to build more and more momentum. But rather than being an instinctual behavior, it was becoming a learned behavior. The fear that Kenny felt inside was the same feeling regardless of whether there was imminent physical danger or just uncomfortableness from being around other students. This was the fear, or absence of love, that Carlos had been warned about.

As new experiences came up, Kenny began to interpret them through past images in his mind, and many of those images were influenced by the behavior of others. Very often, that was not how Carlos would interpret those situations. The feelings that Kenny was generating were not in alignment with the vibrations that Carlos was trying to convey. Once this cycle started, it was hard to reverse. As Kenny mixed past images with current events, he would relive negative emotions from those past images. That would reinforce those patterns to be applied to future experiences.

Carlos sensed that getting Kenny to communicate with him was going to be far more challenging than he had anticipated. The sound vibrations that Kenny was interpreting from the *Land* were drowning out the frequency of love coming from the *Field*. This caused them to become out of sync. Too often, Kenny's focus on past images would create the dominant negative feelings that would offset the positive vibrational frequency of Carlos.

This pattern would continue as he approached his high school years. Kenny's body grew but not at the same rate as others his age. His bright red hair and deep blue eyes couldn't take the attention away from his diminutive five-foot frame, which was more than a foot shorter than his father's frame. Carlos noticed that whenever Kenny's parents had guests come to the house, they too would invariably comment on Kenny's frail physical stature.

"He looks so sickly. Are you sure he's well?"

"Oh yes. He's just fine, thank you," his mother would respond reassuringly.

But Kenny, on overhearing such comments, repeatedly asked himself, *Am I really sick? Why else would I be so small for my age?*

Carlos would try to intervene. "Don't worry. We're healthy! I'm right here with you."

There was never a reply. His pleas didn't seem to get through to his human self. Kenny only focused on the vibrations he received from his physical senses. The more he thought about being sick, the more he believed it. The more he believed it, the more he felt it. He was just tired at first, but then he really started to feel his energy draining. His appetite diminished and he lost more weight. He had a series of infections that appeared to be unrelated. Through each episode, he communicated less and less with his parents. They noticed his change in behavior and appearance and decided to take him for a full medical check-up.

After several blood tests and a chest x-ray, their doctor told Kenny and his parents that they would need to run some more tests. That's when Kenny was convinced there was something very wrong with him. His parents shared his concern. After the second round of tests, they sat nervously in the reception area, waiting for the doctor to return from his examination. The silence was deafening. Kenny stared out the window at the autumn leaves rustling in the wind as his parents remained motionless inside.

"What do you think he's going to find?" his mother finally whispered to his dad.

"Whatever it is, we will get through this together," his father replied reassuringly.

His mother glanced over at Kenny. He didn't say a word but his facial expressions let his mother know that he was worried about what the doctor might say.

"May I get some water?" he asked. She nodded, and he stood up and left the room.

While he was gone, Kenny's doctor entered the room with a concerned look on his face.

"This is not what I was expecting," he began.

"What is it?" Kenny's mother blurted out.

The doctor looked around to see if Kenny was still in the room. When he noticed he was gone, he decided to speak more directly. "We need to run more tests, but the early indications are that Kenny has acute myeloid leukemia."

"Cancer?" his mother gasped.

"Yes. The leukemia cells are what have been causing him to have a harder time fighting off infections."

"Can you treat it?" asked his father.

"We recommend sending Kenny to the best pediatric hospital in the country."

Kenny's parents turned to each other in a state of shock. His father could see tears welling up in his wife's eyes. He turned back towards the doctor while he was still able to share his thoughts. "What hospital is that?" he finally mustered.

"The Hospital for Energy and Radiation Treatment. It's also known as *H.E.A.R.T.*"

His mother buried her face in his father's shoulder and cried.

❦ ❦ ❦

Kenny and his parents sat at the kitchen table eating dinner. They had already discussed all the potential courses of action … none of which made them feel any better. Now there was not much dialogue between the three of them. Everyone was too preoccupied with their own thoughts. Kenny was scared but he tried not to reveal how he was feeling. He could sense the fear that his parents were failing to suppress.

He finally broke the silence. "May I please be excused?"

His mother perked up as if suddenly awoken from a deep sleep. "Yes, of course."

Kenny went into his room but left the door slightly ajar. After sitting on his bed for a brief moment, he slowly walked over and put his ear to the crack in the doorway. Then he listened.

"I'm so scared," he heard his mother admit.

His father tried to reassure her. "Let's not jump to conclusions."

"Jump to conclusions?" she answered incredulously. "He has leukemia, Matt. They're barely giving him a year to live." She tried to suppress her sobs but they were uncontrollable.

Kenny was speechless while he remained frozen in the doorway. His mother's sobs pierced his heart like a Swiss blade knife.

"That's worst-case scenario," his dad declared with little conviction.

Kenny listened for a reply but could only hear his mother's silence.

❦ ❦ ❦

There was little time for the shock to sink in and even less time to act. Leaving the home that had become his sanctuary was another big challenge for Kenny. It was a somber car ride to *H.E.A.R.T.* Kenny understood why he needed to go there. That was not the issue. *Why me?* was the issue. He kept silently repeating those words throughout the trip to the facility. Carlos tried to answer but his messages were not being received by Kenny. He could feel Kenny's energy was drained. Instead of interpreting Carlos's positive vibrations, Kenny stared out the window at the summer scenery flashing by. He was supposed to be starting high school next month and now he wasn't sure if he would ever make it there.

*H.E.A.R.T.* was an innovative treatment and research facility for children and young adults that offered the most advanced and progressive procedures for the treatment of terminal childhood illnesses. It was built on several acres of sprawling green pasture. It projected a peaceful aura on the outside that belied the intensity of the emotions on the inside. Its top team of doctors were at the pinnacle of their profession. The success of their progressive treatments led to substantial fundraising initiatives that allowed them to expand their cutting-edge technology. The patients varied in age and their illnesses varied in severity. In addition to the cluster of buildings where all the treatments were administered, there was a long-term housing facility where the young adult patients took up extended stays if they were projected to undergo treatments lasting longer than three months. This was where Kenny was scheduled to go.

As they pulled up to the main entrance of *H.E.A.R.T.*, Kenny wished he could change his mind. He no longer wanted to be there. The thought, *I don't care if I get better or not*, echoed in his mind. A team of nurses came out to greet him and his parents. They welcomed them in, and made them comfortable inside a rectangular shaped room that was a cross between an office and a living room. A tall, lanky man strolled in while they sipped on flavored ice water. Kenny couldn't help noticing his white beard was camouflaged by the long white coat he was wearing. Behind the beard and the silver glasses, his facial expressions resembled a card player at a blackjack table.

"Hello, Mr. and Mrs. Haneg," he said. "My name is Dr. Milton and I would like to welcome you to the Hospital of Energy and Radiation Treatment." His gaze slid over to Kenny. "Hello, Kenneth. We are going to do everything possible to help get you better so you will eventually be able to go back home with your parents."

"Thank you," Kenny responded in a somber voice. "I would like that very much."

As Dr. Milton was finishing with his overview of the facilities, a dark-haired woman with oval eyes stepped into the back of the room. Her almond-colored dress was simple and neat. She clutched a small note pad in her left hand. Kenny and his parents stood up and were escorted over to the newly arrived woman. She looked directly at Kenny and exuded a warmth that immediately put him at ease.

"Kenny, my name is Miss Martin. My job is to be your single most important point of contact here. Please don't hesitate to ask any questions that you have. Let me take you on a tour of the facilities, as well as show you to your personal accommodations."

Kenny was overwhelmed with emotion. He was staring at Miss Martin but was not able to comprehend everything she was saying. After the long car ride to get there, the fear of the unknown was taking its toll on him. How long would he be here? Would he ever leave? So many questions. Very few answers.

Over the course of the next two days, Miss Martin introduced Kenny and his parents to a slew of doctors, nurses and administrative staff. She explained the treatments that Kenny would be getting and what he should expect from his stay at the facility. Carlos knew that if he could get through to Kenny, this would be a temporary stay. Kenny was not so confident.

# CHAPTER 4
# A VISITOR IN THE NIGHT

The daily routine at *H.E.A.R.T.* was just as Miss Martin had described. There were days that Kenny would rather forget. The most intense medical treatments were powerful and unforgiving on his body. Those were the times he felt even sicker than when he'd arrived. Other days, he was more attentive and the staff were there to keep him preoccupied with varying activities. He was introduced to a few other patients but he largely kept to himself.

*Why bother?* he thought. *I'm not going to be here long anyway.*

He went through the motions of day-to-day life at *H.E.A.R.T.* but nothing seemed to shake his melancholy feeling. Even the life specialist who was assigned to Kenny had trouble introducing him to different teen activities while he was between treatments. He reluctantly participated in a few of them. There were rooms with state-of-the-art visual effects – but they didn't have the desired effect of lifting his spirits.

Early one afternoon, Kenny sat in his room getting ready for his parents to come back. As he looked around, he at least felt appreciation that he was able to secure a room in the long-term housing facility at *H.E.A.R.T.* His bed felt more personal to him than one of the standard hospital beds, and he often sat at the small rectangular desk where he could doodle and draw pictures from his imagination. In the corner of the room, a black chair faced towards the window and overlooked a small courtyard that Kenny rarely paid any attention to. As soon as his parents came into his room, he sensed there was something different about their demeanor but he couldn't identify it. His mother seemed to be suppressing a smile.

"Is everything okay?" he asked with heightened curiosity.

"Oh yes," his mother answered before the rest of her smile broke out across her face. "We have some very good news to share with you."

Kenny was intrigued. This was not something he was expecting but the anticipation of the news felt good to him and he didn't want to let that feeling go. He smiled back at her and waited a brief moment before replying, "Well, are you going to share?"

His mother glanced over at his father and he gave her an approving nod. She took a deep breath and said, "It looks like you're going to have a baby sister."

Kenny had to let the words sink in. There was a cascade of thoughts and emotions that he was trying to process and they were all joyous. "Finally!" he shouted. He had always imagined what it would be like to have a sibling, but he'd never brought it up to his parents because he didn't want them to feel bad if they couldn't have any more children. But now it didn't matter. He was going to be a big brother!

Lying in bed that night, Kenny couldn't stop thinking about the great news he'd received during the day. The more he thought about the new sister he would soon have, the more excitement built up inside of him. He visualized playing with her. He was so happy that he felt like he was going to jump out of his skin.

"I can't believe this. I'm going to have a baby sister! I wish I could share this with someone," he said with pure delight.

Carlos was listening and responded with his usual encouragement. "You can."

"What?" Kenny exclaimed out loud.

*What just happened?* thought Carlos. *Did Kenny just respond to me?*

There was a pause.

Then Carlos answered again. "You can."

"I can what?" said Kenny.

"Share your joy with me."

"Who are you?"

After another pause, Carlos responded, "I am you."

"What do you mean, 'I am you'?" Kenny asked with a great deal of confusion. His heart pounded. He shook his head violently as if to scare away the voice.

"I am you," Carlos repeated from within.

"Where did you come from?"

"The *Field… of Potential Probabilities.*"

"What's that?"

"It's a field of energy."

Kenny was in disbelief. Again, he tried to collect his thoughts. He decided to continue. "You're saying I came from a field of energy?"

"Yes."

"Where is this field?"

"Everywhere."

Kenny instinctively glanced around the room as if to look for this voice he was communicating with. "What are you doing here?"

"I was always here."

Kenny raised his eyebrows. "How come I never knew that?"

"You just couldn't communicate with me."

"Why can I communicate with you now?" Kenny asked.

"Because you can feel me."

Kenny rubbed his fingertips together while opening and closing his hands. "You mean I communicate with you through feelings?"

"Yes."

"That still doesn't explain why I can communicate with you now, but I couldn't communicate with you yesterday."

"Your little sister."

A smile returned to Kenny's face. "What about her? I can't wait until she's born."

"That feeling of joy and excitement you have about her is what caused you to be able to raise your vibrations so that you could feel me," Carlos explained.

"So, I can only reach you when I feel joy and excitement?"

"That's the best way to reach me."

"What is this … I'm your body or something?"

"Yes. You are the physical version of me. I wanted to experience myself, so I got to come here as you."

Kenny straightened up. "Why did you want to do that?"

"I wanted to feel what it was like to be me in a physical body and get to experience love and joy through you."

"It's not all love and joy, you know," said Kenny.

"Yes, I know," replied Carlos. "I want to experience all the feelings you go through."

"Why did you pick me? I'm stuck in this hospital. Don't you want to experience love and joy through someone who's healthy and running around outside?"

"There are a lot of people running around your world with far less love and joy than you have right here and now. I can experience love and joy as long as you're willing to give it."

"I'm willing to give it, but I don't have much time left. I have a terminal illness, you know."

"What is a terminal illness?" Carlos questioned him.

"It means I'm going to die soon."

"Everyone is going to die," said Carlos. "Death just means your dash is going to complete itself. Your concept of a terminal illness is attempting to put a timeframe on the completion of your dash."

"What are you talking about? What's a dash?"

"Let's just say it's the full amount of time you spend here on Gaia."

"Whatever. I'm just telling you what the doctors told me."

"I'm not concerned about what the doctors told you," Carlos replied.

"Why not?"

"Because I came here to feel what it's like to be me."

"Sorry to disappoint you, but now you have to feel what it's like to be me."

"Yes, but you can be me too," Carlos countered.

"I'm confused," Kenny confessed. "Is this my journey to get to know you, or is it your journey to get to know me?"

"Both," said Carlos. "And as long as you are aware of your breath and can feel my love, then we are in sync and get to share this journey together."

"Well, get ready for a short journey," Kenny cautioned.

"Why is that?"

"You're forgetting, I'm going to die soon."

Carlos knew this was a crucial opportunity to share his wisdom with Kenny. "There you go using that word again. What is 'soon'?"

"It means there's not much time left."

"What is time?" Carlos asked.

"Ummm … you know, it's on the clock. It's how we measure how long we are here on Gaia."

"What happens to time when you leave Gaia?"

Kenny rolled his eyes. "I don't know. I never thought about it."

"Time doesn't exist in the way that you think it does," said Carlos. "Sure, you can measure how much time it takes you to do something or how long it takes you to move from one place to another while you are here. But whenever you look at time, it is always the same."

"What do you mean?"

"It is always 'now'."

"It's not always now," said Kenny.

"When is it not now?"

"Yesterday is not now. Tomorrow is not now."

Carlos was enjoying this dialogue. "When it was yesterday, was it now?

"I suppose …," said Kenny uncertainly.

"When it is tomorrow, will it be now?"

"Well, yeah. I guess so."

"It is so," said Carlos. "It is always now, but every new 'now' is more expansive than the one before it. You think of it as linear, like going backwards to past time, or going forward to future time, but it is always now … and if it is always the same time, then time is really not linear. You have a physical body here on Gaia, but you don't physically go back and forth in time. Correct?"

"That's right," agreed Kenny. "So ... what is time?"

"Since it is always now, time is just a measurement you use to differentiate between your perception of reality."

Kenny frowned. "Perception of reality?"

"Let me see how I can explain this better."

There was a pause. Carlos was excited he was finally in direct communion with his human self, so he wanted to make sure that Kenny could understand the messages he was trying to convey.

"Think of your life as a movie," Carlos continued. "Your perception is the lens through which you watch the movie of your life. And your reality is that movie come to life. What you believe to be true in any moment of your life is based on what you think and how you feel. Those are the vibrations that you project out into the world. As a result, that is what you attract back into your life and that is what you experience."

"What do you mean by vibrations?"

"Everything is vibrations, but let me simplify," said Carlos. "There is a physical reality, which is the world you can see, and touch, and hear. And then there is a non-physical world, or vibrational reality that you cannot feel with your physical senses."

"Is that world real?" Kenny asked.

"What do you think? That's where we came from."

Kenny wasn't sure what he was thinking. "Are you real or just in my imagination?"

"What do you think your imagination is?"

"It's what I'm thinking, I guess," Kenny replied without much conviction.

"Okay, so it's just a collection of your thoughts. Where do you think those thoughts go?"

Kenny looked around. "I don't know. I never thought about it."

"A thought is just a vibration stored as energy in the *Field of Potential Probabilities*."

Now Kenny was really confused. "I'm not sure I understand."

"That *Field of Potential Probabilities* is where we came from. We can call it the *Field*. So that just means that all your thoughts are collected and stored in the *Field*."

"What happens to them?"

"All those thoughts are waiting to turn into things that you can see and feel in the *Land of Perception and Time*."

"Where's this *Land of Perception and Time*?" Kenny continued.

"You're living in it. You call it Gaia."

"Why do you call it the Land of Perception and Time?"

"In the *Field*, there is no concept of time like you have here. But we get to watch and observe these *Lands*."

"'These Lands'?" Kenny repeated. "You mean there's more than one Gaia?"

'You don't think there's more than one?" asked Carlos.

"I just assumed …."

"In a universe of trillions of planets, you just assumed that yours is the only one with living organisms? That's like saying, 'What? I have more than one cell in my body?' In that case, my response would be the same. In a body of trillions of cells, why would you assume you only have one, and why would you assume they can't communicate with each other?"

*This is really getting weird*, Kenny thought to himself. *What the heck is going on?*

As doubts stirred through his head, his conversation with Carlos ended as swiftly as it had begun.

The next day, Kenny kept thinking about his conversation from the previous night. He didn't dare mention it to anyone because he knew he would be ridiculed. Still, he couldn't get the thought of it out of his mind. Later that night, Kenny tried to reach out to whomever that had been the night before.

"Are you still there?" he asked with some trepidation.

No response.

*I knew it wasn't real,* he thought to himself. But as he sat up in bed, he kept wishing that he hadn't just imagined it.

Then he remembered what he'd done. He started to think about how it would feel to have a new baby sister. He got goosebumps with excitement, just like the night before. He turned his attention to his imaginary visitor.

"Hello?" he said out loud.

"Hello," Carlos responded internally.

"Wow, you're back."

"Yes, I am."

"I have so many questions."

"Then fire away." Carlos was ecstatic to be able to communicate with Kenny again.

"You don't mind?"

"The only way you'll get answers is if you ask questions."

Kenny nodded to his invisible companion. "Let's start with what I should call you."

"You can call me Carlos."

"That works for me, but how do I know it's you answering me? How do I know the difference between your voice and mine?"

"If you want to understand me, you have to know which frequency I'm on...and which language I speak. You can understand other people talk by tuning into their sound vibrations with your ears, and then learning the language they speak. If they speak Spanish but you only understand English, then you can hear the sound vibrations but do not understand the language. For you and me to be in communion, you must tune into a different frequency than the sound vibrations you are accustomed to. You must also know the language that I use."

"What language is that?" asked Kenny.

"The language of feelings."

"But how do I understand your words?"

"My language is universal. It doesn't use words."

"How do I understand it?" Kenny persisted.

"Just listen to it. If you tune into me, then you can interpret the vibrations I am sending you. Likewise, your feelings are the language that I understand."

"My feelings?"

"Yes."

Kenny felt a strange sensation in his gut. "How do you know how I'm feeling?"

"I can feel the frequency."

"But what about my thoughts? Doesn't it matter what I'm thinking?"

"Of course," said Carlos. "Your thoughts are a frequency too. But your emotions are even more important."

"Soooo…if my thoughts and emotions are so important, why did you say that my feelings were the language you understand?"

"Your feelings are simply the result of your thoughts plus your emotions. Depending on which emotion you attach to each thought, you create a new feeling state. The feeling tells me what you really desire."

"That could get very confusing. How many different emotions can I have?"

"Two."

"What?"

"That's right. Only two," confirmed Carlos. "Love and fear."

Kenny was still confused. "Why are there only two emotions?"

"You can really say there is only one emotion."

"How can you say that?"

"There is the emotion of love and there is the absence of it. You call that fear. In the same manner, you can say there is no such thing as darkness. There is only light."

Kenny disagreed. "But there is darkness."

"Darkness is just a name you use to describe the absence of light. As long as there is light, there is no such thing as darkness. Only when you turn off the light can darkness reveal itself. Otherwise, it does not exist. Likewise, as long as there is love, there is no such thing as fear. Only when you cut off the feeling of love can fear reveal itself. Otherwise, it does not exist."

"Is that the same as my feelings?"

Carlos was pleased with where the conversation was going. "Either emotion coupled with a thought produces a range of feeling states. You look at them as good or bad. We don't. We just look at them as love-based or fear-based."

"How many feeling states are there?"

"More than you can count. But the only one that matters is the one that you are feeling right now."

"That reminds me," said Kenny. "Last night you got me really confused when you were talking about time."

"In the *Field of Potential Probabilities*, everything is happening all at once. But here in the *Land of Perception and Time*, you are focused on only one potential probability at a time.

"Why do you keep calling this the *Land of Perception and Time*?"

"Because you allow your experience here to be dictated by perception and time."

Kenny was trying to remember everything he had been told. "Can you explain that again?"

"In any moment, your experience of life is determined by the lens through which you observe it. That is your perception. If you see through the same lens that we are observing your life, you will be filled with appreciation and joy regardless of your physical circumstances. But if you choose to observe your life through the lens of others, then it is much harder to feel the satisfaction of being in alignment with us in the *Field*. When that happens, your experience of life, or your perception of reality, will be much different.

"Of course, I want to be in alignment with you," said Kenny.

"That's great to hear because that is the first step. The lens is the key. Knowing which lens you are observing your life through is so much simpler than you realize, since there are only two lenses. The *Lens of Love* means you are aware of your connection to the *Field* and the *Lens of Fear* means you are not aware of your connection to the *Field*."

"I want to observe the movie of my life through the Lens of Love."

"Then watch that movie, Kenny. I am right here with you, looking through your eyes."

"If you're looking through my eyes, then how do I see through your lens?"

"Even though we are non-physical beings and you are physical beings, we are still connected. It is the same with everything around you. Your science teachings refer to physical things as matter and non-physical things, like us, as energy. Matter is perceived as your physical reality and energy is perceived as your vibrational reality. But everything that is in your physical reality already existed in your vibrational reality before it became matter.

"Okay. That's very confusing. Can you go a little slower?" Kenny pleaded.

Carlos tried again. "Everything you ever experience in your physical world already exists in the *Field* as a potential probability. The lens through which you observe it – the *Lens of Love* or the *Lens of Fear* – determines which potential probability will manifest into your perception of reality."

"That really wasn't less confusing. You know that, right?"

"Sorry. I'm trying to keep this at a level where you can understand. Take in what you can and don't worry about the rest. Eventually it will all start to make more sense."

"I certainly hope so," said Kenny. "I'm still trying to figure out where you even came from."

"I told you, we came from the *Field*. But let me go over *why* we came. Before I came into your physical body, I knew that there would be a lot of things that I would want to do once we started to experience the physical realm. There were two things that I knew ahead of time that I wanted to do with you more than anything else. One of them, we do all of the time and one of them, we do some of the time, but you are rarely aware of us doing them. So, I guess my biggest 'ask' of you is to try to be consciously aware of doing these two things as much as you can."

"Sure. Just tell me what these two things are that you came here to do."

"One of them is to keep breathing, otherwise we can't stay here."

"I get that. Don't worry, I'm always breathing," said Kenny.

"Yes, but you are not always aware of your breath."

Kenny disagreed. "What are you talking about? I know I'm breathing right now."

"There is a difference between knowing that you are breathing ... and being consciously aware of each breath."

"Okay, I will try to be consciously aware of each breath. What's the other thing?" Kenny asked impatiently.

"I want to feel what it's like to *Be Me*."

Kenny surveyed the room as if he would find Carlos sitting there. "Hmmm ... and how do you suggest we do that?"

"Just feel love."

"I try to do that but sometimes it's not so easy."

"Yes, I know. It's not so easy because of everything going on around you in your life."

"Exactly," agreed Kenny.

"What I want you to know is that you can feel love regardless of what is going on in your life. That is all we felt in the *Field of Potential Probabilities*. That is what we will feel when we go back. That is what we came to feel while we are here. It is a decision. It is a choice ... and it is not dependent on anything or anyone else."

"I know what I want to choose ... but I have a lot of different feelings and it's hard to control them sometimes," Kenny admitted.

"All of your feeling states are derived from whether you feel love or not. If you feel love then you are in sync with me. If you do not feel love then you have forgotten about our connection and we are out of sync."

"Okay, I will give it a try. My intention is that I will be conscious of my breath and I will be conscious of feeling love. That's the best that I can do."

"Thank you," replied Carlos. "This is why we came here!"

❧  ❧  ❧

It was hard for Kenny to keep his conversations with Carlos a secret. He started becoming more friendly with a number of the other patients and he was tempted to say something about Carlos but he didn't want to scare them away. In the meantime, he still had so many questions to ask and he didn't want to jeopardize his ability to communicate with him. Early in the morning became his favorite time to reach Carlos. He found himself getting up earlier and earlier, and each morning he would climb out of bed and sit in the black cushioned chair looking towards the back courtyard.

Initially, it took some time for their communication to begin. Eventually, Kenny was able to come into alignment with Carlos with relative ease. He would sit up straight and keep thinking of a past conversation that he'd had with Carlos. Once he replayed that dialogue in his mind a few times, he was able to create a new dialogue as he focused on his breath. One morning he found himself thinking about when he was healthy.

"Are you there?"

"Yes," responded Carlos.

Kenny felt a wave of excitement run through his body. "Good. I have some more unresolved questions."

"What would you like to ask me?"

"Why me? Why am I sick? What did I do to deserve this?"

"That is a very fair question and there is probably no answer that will completely satisfy you."

"That's not helpful."

"Let me ask you a question, Kenny. Do you want to get better?"

"Of course, I do."

"Do you expect to get better?"

"I don't know. I hope I do."

"How do you expect to get better if you don't expect to get better?"

The question surprised Kenny. "I never looked at it that way."

"The expectation must come first."

"What do you mean?"

"You must experience the expectation of healing before the healing can occur. You can't have the healing first and then the expectation. It is the expectation that creates the healing."

Kenny could feel his shoulders start to slump. "You lost me."

"Let's look at it a different way," said Carlos. "Imagine that you have gone through all the challenges with your physical illness, and then you end up walking out that front door of *H.E.A.R.T.* completely healthy. Think of how that would feel."

"Okay."

"How does it feel?"

"It feels sweet!" Kenny answered with a smirk.

"Now imagine that you were always healthy from birth and you never experienced being sick. Do you think you could have the same appreciation of being healthy as you do if you overcome major sickness?"

"Of course not."

"Well, now you have a greater opportunity to experience that heightened level of joy and appreciation than someone who was always healthy."

"Nice try," Kenny replied dryly. "I would be just fine if I'd always been healthy. Besides, what if I don't get better?"

"You will get better when you are no longer capable of asking that question."

"I *am* asking that question! What if I don't get healed?"

"You are already healed," Carlos reassured him.

"How can you tell me that I'm already healed? I am not healed! I'm not in this hospital because I am well. In case you didn't notice, they only admit people into this hospital who are not well!"

"You are not well because you have been told you are not well and you believe that to be true. That is different than the possibility of being well."

Kenny could feel his blood pressure starting to rise. "I don't want the possibility of being well. I want the reality to be well!"

"Then believe that you are."

"Okay. I believe I can get better. Am I better now?" asked Kenny sarcastically.

"No," replied Carlos.

"Why not? You just said if I believe it, I will get better."

"Yes, I said if you believe it. But you don't believe it. You said it, but you don't believe it. In order to believe it, you need to feel as if it can come true."

"I want to believe it. So how can I feel something if I don't think it can come true?"

"You have to start small. You have to believe something is going to happen where you don't already have such strong feelings that it won't happen. When that comes true, then you do it again and again. Little baby steps, but each step will give you confidence that what you think and feel will result in what you see."

Kenny took a few slow deep breaths as he contemplated what Carlos was trying to explain. He remembered the first time that he'd thought about playing the guitar. He'd never expected to be able to play the instrument. But during a series of lessons, his instructor had kept telling him, "You will be able to play. Take baby steps. It's all about baby steps." After much repetition and practice, he had become proficient at playing the guitar.

"You're saying I need to expect it to happen?" It was more of a statement than a question.

Carlos was pleased. "You always get what you expect, whether you like it or not. If you don't like what you see, it's not that you didn't get what you expected; you just need to change your expectation."

"Wait. You lost me again." This time it was more of a question than a statement.

Carlos shifted the point he was trying to make. "There are many times you expect what you don't want."

"Why would I do that?" asked Kenny.

"It may be based on what other people told you, or your interpretation of things you have seen. So you expect something similar for yourself, even if it's what you don't want. Then when it comes to pass, you think it was out of your control, but you were the one who created it by your expectation."

"Okay. So how do I change my expectation to something that I want? I want to expect to be healthy, but when I ask myself, 'Do I expect to be healthy?' I feel resistance. A lot of times I feel fear. I can't help it. So how do I overcome that fear so I can expect to be healthy?"

"*Now* you are starting to ask the right questions."

"Then start giving me the right answers!" Kenny retorted.

"When you know something to be true, that is when you start to expect it," said Carlos. "Let me try to explain it another way. Everything you know to be true is based on what has happened in the past. You refer to that as the known … and it is easy for you to believe in the known. But the past, or the known, is just an image you have in your mind. What you believe is what you will see. Therefore, that is what becomes true for you in the future. On the other hand, everything that is possible in the future is the unknown. It is much more challenging for you to believe in the unknown because your senses haven't validated it yet."

Kenny nodded. "I would agree with that."

"Forget about what your senses have validated," Carlos stated emphatically. "The *Field* is full of potential probabilities … and being healthy is one of them. So, imagine yourself to be healthy. I can only tell you that if you look into the unknown, and you believe what you imagine to be true, that is what we will see."

Kenny closed his eyes and started to imagine how it would feel to be healthy.

⚜ ⚜ ⚜

The cafeteria at *H.E.A.R.T.* was a large open space with small tables spaciously spread out to afford plenty of room for wheelchairs or groups of people to walk by. Each table was accompanied by four bright-colored chairs. Kenny used the cafeteria as a form of sanctuary to sit by himself in a different setting. An added bonus was that he enjoyed the food and the atmosphere of the café. He especially liked to sit down and eat a snack late in the afternoon when few other people were around. On this particular day, he clutched a cup of vanilla frozen yogurt as he walked past another teen who was sitting at a table by himself.

"Have a seat," said the patient in a barely audible voice as he looked up at Kenny.

Kenny instinctively halted his progress. He preferred to eat alone but he was also not accustomed to being asked to join another patient.

He looked down at the young man staring back at him and said, "Sure."

"My name is James," said the teen.

"Hi, I'm Kenny," he responded hesitantly.

As he sat down, he felt the warmth of James's smile that had not been apparent to him earlier. Kenny noticed a small processor behind each of James's ears.

"What are those for?" he asked as he motioned towards James's ear.

"They're cochlear implants. They let me hear."

Kenny kept staring at them. "Is that why you're in here?"

"I wish," James responded. "No, I also have a bad heart. How about you?"

"Cancer. But I don't know how good my heart is either."

James studied his face to see if he was serious or just kidding. Kenny's smile gave James his answer. James felt at ease and returned his smile. They continued talking as if they had known each other for a long time. They shared stories of growing up and how they had come to be here at *H.E.A.R.T.* There was a comfortableness about James that Kenny hadn't felt with anyone else. It was nice to have a friend at *H.E.A.R.T.*

As the days progressed, Kenny and Carlos fell into a more comfortable routine of communication. Each night, they would go over the details of that day, and each morning, Kenny would wake up in anticipation of connecting with Carlos.

Before going to bed one evening, Kenny started a new conversation.

"One of the patients was talking about his soul today. When I asked him about it, he couldn't really explain it except for saying it was inside of him."

"That is correct," Carlos confirmed.

"You're inside of me. Does that mean you're my soul?"

"You can call me that."

"I know I can call you that, but is that really who you are?"

"I am whatever you would like me to be."

"Again, not really helpful."

"I like your sense of humor."

"I didn't know I was being funny," Kenny replied without a smile. "I'm trying to figure out who this invisible thing I'm talking to is, and you find humor in it."

"Never take your life experience too seriously. If you knew how excited we were to be coming here, you wouldn't let anything bother you."

"I wouldn't know," said Kenny. "So, what determines whether one of you gets to come here on Gaia, anyway?"

"A lottery."

"You're kidding, right?"

"No, I'm not."

"C'mon. Seriously, how do you get picked to come here?"

"A lottery," repeated Carlos.

"I didn't realize things were so sophisticated in this *Field* of yours."

"Sometimes simpler is better."

Kenny frowned. "So, they just put everyone's name in a hat and pick out a winner?"

"Not everyone."

"What do you mean? Not all eternal beings can come here?"

"They can all come here but they don't *have* to come here. They must *want* to come here in order to get into the lottery. The ones who haven't chosen to come here are always supporting those who do come."

Kenny nodded in approval.

"Like I said," said Carlos, "sometimes simpler is better."

"Speaking of simpler, can you explain more simply how you were talking about everyone's dash? This is our lives, right?"

"Yes, you can look at it that way."

"What about before there were any dashes?"

"You mean before there were human beings on Gaia?"

"Yeah. What was it like back then?" asked Kenny.

"Let's start by looking at the evolution of time on your planet." Carlos proceeded to tell him what it was like to watch all the different *Lands* from the *Field*. He told Kenny about Gaia and how they watched the formation of the planet through each of the different eons. Kenny was fascinated. He fell asleep that night dreaming about the formation of different planets.

# Chapter 5
## "Be Carlos for a Day"

After a full dose of chemotherapy, Kenny was feeling particularly nauseated and worn down. This was not unusual at *H.E.A.R.T.* Each of the patients seemed to take turns going through rough patches. Headaches, nausea, fatigue, and worse … these were common side effects which they all learned to deal with in their own way. Kenny was no different.

He found himself sleeping a lot and not having communication with Carlos. This went on for a few days. One saving grace was that each time he opened his eyes, there was an angel staring back at him. It was his mother. He would look deep into her sky-blue eyes and feel her love and compassion reflecting back to him. In those moments, he couldn't imagine what she was going through. He was too consumed with trying to survive himself. She was steady as a rock, but through the warmth she was projecting, he could sense a pain she was trying to conceal. He didn't know if a heart could break, but looking at his mother, he realized what it would look like if it could.

In the meantime, Carlos was doing everything he could to try and cheer him up. Those were the times where Carlos felt he could provide the most help, but he wasn't able to get through. After several days, Kenny started to feel better and he sat up in bed watching television. He was laughing at one of his favorite shows when the thought of Carlos popped into his mind and he asked out loud, "Are you there?"

"Aren't I always here?" Carlos answered.

Kenny chuckled. "I guess you are."

Carlos was pleased that Kenny had intentionally reached out to him again. "I'm glad to see you are having fun."

"Fun?" Kenny replied with more than a little frustration. "I wouldn't exactly call this fun. How am I supposed to have fun when I'm so sick?"

"I understand this is difficult," said Carlos, "but there is always another perspective."

"And just what is that?"

"If fun comes from things in the *Land of Perception and Time*, then it is always conditional. If fun comes from your alignment with me in the *Field*, then it is unconditional and can come at any time. I came here to have fun with you, Kenny. When you truly realize that, then we can have fun together regardless of what is going on around you."

"You mean having fun like when I'm just playing with one of my friends?"

"Exactly. Our fun is in the alignment of you and me. The fun doesn't come first and then our alignment. The alignment comes first and then the fun always follows."

"I suppose you always had fun when you were in the *Field*."

"Yes, we always have fun there," confirmed Carlos.

"Why do you call it *The Field of Potential Probabilities*?"

"If there is the potential for something to happen, it does not mean that you will experience it happening. It only means that it *could* happen."

"What good is that?"

Carlos shifted directions. "If one person out of one million got cured of a terminal illness, would you agree there is the potential for it to happen?"

Kenny shrugged. "I guess so."

"Then if there is the potential for something to happen, what is the determining factor of whether it happens or not?"

"Whatever the odds are. You know, one in a thousand … one in a million.…"

"Wrong answer."

"Then what is it?" asked Kenny.

"Let me give you a hint: belief."

"Whether I believe it's possible or not?"

"Yes, and not only that, but whether you can *feel as if it can happen*! Remember, if you truly believe in something, you feel as if it has already happened. Likewise, if you have a desire, I have already figured out how to make it come true. That desire coming true is now a potential probability waiting to come true in this field of energy that you have access to. You just have to align with it. If you doubt it, you are not in alignment with it, and you will not be able to experience that potential. If you believe it in your heart, you are in resonance with that potential, and you can start attracting it to you."

Kenny was trying to believe it. "I hear you, but it's still hard to imagine that this *Field* is real."

"Just because you can't see it or touch it now doesn't mean it's not real. It's a vibration and all vibrations are real. In fact, everything you can see and touch is still a vibration. Tell me, which vibration or potential probability would you like to experience: staying sick or becoming well?"

"What kind of question is that?" said Kenny. "Of course, I want to experience becoming well!"

"Then understand that your experience of being well is waiting for you. You are the sole determining factor of whether you will experience it or not."

"But…"

"When you say 'but' you have just introduced doubt back into your thoughts and emotions, and shifted your potential probability from wellness to the absence of it. Now you no longer believe it."

"I'm just being realistic," Kenny countered. "Everyone in here is here for a reason. They're sick and they're probably not leaving. Why am I different?"

"You are no different from anyone else. Every one of you can believe what you are told to be true, and accept that as your reality ... or you can believe in what you wish to be true and allow that to become your reality."

"You make it sound so simple but it's not!"

"Think of it this way," Carlos continued. "You are all farmers, planting the seeds of your wellness. The feeling of joy and appreciation that your wellness is coming is the nourishment for your seeds. But when you sprinkle doubt all over the seeds, you cut off the nourishment of that desire for wellness, and it can no longer grow."

"But what if I share this with others and they tell me I'm crazy for believing this?"

"If you plant seeds in your backyard and you are convinced that it will produce beautiful flowers, it doesn't matter what your neighbors believe. They can tell you, 'That's stupid. You'll never be able to grow flowers there.' But as long as *you* expect the seeds to produce flowers, and you keep 'watering' those seeds, they will produce beautiful flowers even if you can't see those flowers right now."

Kenny let those words sink in for a little while before responding. "I'll try to keep watering the seeds of wellness. Okay?"

"That's all that I ask."

During the day, Kenny tried eating in the community cafeteria as much as possible. It gave him time to be around some of the other patients. He enjoyed the contrast of personalities between the different patients but none of them could lift his spirits like Stevie could. Stevie was small in physical stature, like Kenny, but was always the most optimistic person in the room. Her red and blue bandana could easily be spotted wrapped around her head. Whenever any of the other patients started to feel down, she shifted the conversation to something positive. She lifted all of their spirits.

Kenny walked into the cafeteria and he immediately noticed that there was no bandana to be found. Stevie was not going to be joining him for lunch. He tried to hide his disappointment as he sat down next to a few other patients. They exchanged some small talk but mostly sat in silence. Kenny wanted to engage in conversation with the others but couldn't come up with the right words to share. Without Stevie's positive influence, the lack of communication just made him pull away from the others even further.

He went back to his room and began to think about how he had ended up at *H.E.A.R.T.* Dormant thoughts started to resurface and he suddenly felt trapped in the hospital with no way out. He went to sleep that night with the hope that he would wake up feeling better. Instead, he woke up a short time later only feeling worse. He felt a wave of panic overcoming his body.

"Help! Help! Help!" he kept repeating to himself in bed.

Carlos heard his pleas and tried to help.

"Breathe!" Carlos pleaded. "Breathe. Feel your breath!"

It went back and forth like dueling banjos in the night. The more Kenny kept thinking *Help! Help! Help!* Carlos would respond with the instructions, "Breathe! Breathe! Breathe!"

Without any advance warning, Kenny started to focus on his breath. He felt himself taking in deep breaths and slowly exhaling after holding his breath for a few seconds.

"Yes!" shouted Carlos. "*That's* what you're supposed to do!"

After the intense emotional stress that Kenny had just been feeling, the steady focus on his breath finally relaxed him into a deep sleep.

The next morning, he sat in his black chair for a while as he looked around his room. He studied the automated bed that allowed him to sit up comfortably or recline into a flatter sleeping position. Then he shifted his focus to the picture of his parents and himself next to his bed. He thought about how amazing they have been ... sticking by his side through every ordeal and challenge. It couldn't be easy on them. Finally, he turned his attention to Carlos. "Thanks for the help last night."

"That's what I'm here for," Carlos answered.

"It's getting so hard to listen to the other patients. I have a good feeling inside after you and I talk in the morning, but then it gets really challenging when I sit with the other guys. I feel their pain too. I'm not blaming anything on them. This is just so hard for all of us."

Carlos understood how challenging it was for Kenny to get treatments and then go through a form of self-isolation. He wanted to teach Kenny to keep remembering him throughout the day, practicing repetition in order to make it a habit. This would help Kenny create a new program to run constantly in his subconscious mind. If he could do that, then Kenny would be less inclined to hang out in his room trying to escape the constant feeling of anxiety that he felt throughout the day.

"Kenny," Carlos started. "The more you focus on me, the more you will notice me … and the more we can feel the love and joy we came here to experience."

"I'm trying, but it's hard to focus on you when I'm not here in my room. I wish I had my black chair in the Community Room so I could reach you when I'm around the others."

"You don't need your black chair to reach me. You can reach me anytime," Carlos assured him.

"But this is the only time you ever come to me."

"I don't have to come to you, Kenny. I am always with you, so I never leave. The black chair is like your training wheels. You need to believe that ever since you learned how to be in communication with me, you don't need the training wheels any longer."

"I just never think about communicating with you when we're outside this room," said Kenny, "but I'd like to."

"There are no boundaries to where you can communicate with me," Carlos explained. "You can meditate anywhere you want."

"Who said anything about meditation?" Kenny asked.

"You use meditation to access your imagination."

"So …."

"When you use your imagination, you are reaching me in the *Field*."

Kenny was trying to understand. "How do I do that?"

"You already know how. When you were a child, you would play in the *Field* even though you were here on Gaia. We really enjoyed it."

Kenny's frustration started to grow. "I don't remember what you're talking about."

"Do you remember playing with your train set?" Carlos prodded.

"Yes!" Kenny shouted with a sense of relief. "That was so much fun. We traveled all over the country on that train. But it wasn't real."

"It was real for you, so that is what you experienced."

Kenny smiled as he recalled those fond memories. "I did some crazy stuff with my imagination back then. Why did it ever stop?"

"You started paying more attention to your physical senses. As you did, you forgot about using your imagination and then we both stopped experiencing it in the *Field*."

"Are you saying that as soon as I use my imagination, then you get to experience it in the *Field*?"

"*We* experience it…and not just in the *Field*. If you imagine something to be true, and feel what it would be like to experience it, you will experience in the *Land* what you already imagined to be true in the *Field*."

"Really," said Kenny. "Most people would have a hard time believing that their imagination can actually become real."

"I don't know who you mean by 'most people'. I only know that I am you. And by using your imagination, you are just doing the energy work first."

"The energy work….?" Kenny let those words linger as a question.

"Everything is energy, Kenny. If you want to experience change, you can wait until something manifests and then try to change the physical manifestation. That takes time, from your perspective. The alternative is that you can change it energetically…which happens instantaneously. Then you can watch the unfolding of what has already been changed in your imagination."

"I want that to happen. Why can't I remember to do that?"

"Because you are so focused on taking in everything from all around you. You're always downloading incredible amounts of information. You're subconsciously going on auto-pilot, utilizing all the information you have been downloading throughout your life. I was always there trying to communicate with you but you just weren't paying attention to me. Now, when you leave this room, you are running on those same programs you downloaded years ago."

"I'm not trying to ignore you," said Kenny. "I wish I could pay more attention to you."

"I know you do."

"So how do I do that? I really want to know."

"Okay. Then let's play a game," Carlos suggested.

"What's the game?"

"It's called 'Be Carlos for a Day'."

"You want me to be you for a day? I thought I already *am* you."

"You are ... but you keep forgetting it. Then you keep going back to feeling negative emotions based on everyone and everything you see around you. But everybody likes to play games. Don't you?"

"Sure," Kenny agreed.

"Well, the easiest way to keep remembering that I'm right here with you is to make it a game. The easier it is to play, the less resistance to me you put up. That's why the feeling of ease is so important."

"Why would I resist you?"

"You don't do it intentionally, but you don't intentionally pay attention to me either. You're just so trained to focus on what you see, and what other people say. So you base your feelings on what *was*. Instead, focus on me and what we *can be*."

"Don't you ever look at *what was*?"

"No. I never look backwards."

Kenny had a flashback to their discussion on time. "How about *what is*?" he said confidently. "Isn't it important to be aware of what is happening right now?"

"Being aware of right now is very different from focusing on *what is*. Even when you think you are looking at *what is*, you are really looking at *what was*."

Kenny wasn't so confident any more. "And how is that?"

"Because everything you see has already manifested, so its creation has already preceded this moment."

"Say that again."

"There is only now. That means there are only two realities: everything that has manifested before right now…and everything that is in the process of manifesting right now. The real question is: which are you focusing on?"

"I thought I was focusing on *what is*…but I guess I was really focusing on *what was*."

"Correct," confirmed Carlos.

Kenny chuckled. "That's good. I don't even know what I am saying."

"Don't worry, it's going to take a little practice."

"It's going to take a *lot* of practice," corrected Kenny. "So how do we play this game?"

"You just show me around," replied Carlos.

"What do you mean I just show you around? I thought you can see through my eyes."

"Yes, I can, but if you're not paying attention to me, it doesn't do us much good."

"What does me showing you around do?"

"If you keep asking me, 'What do you think of this?' or 'What do you think of that?'…you will be waiting for an answer. Then I know I can communicate with you."

Kenny nodded. "I can do that."

⚜ ⚜ ⚜

The most challenging thing next to being a patient at H.E.A.R.T. was being a parent of a patient at H.E.A.R.T. It was no different for

Kenny's parents. They settled into the unsettling routine of driving back and forth to H.E.A.R.T. on a regular basis. Matt Haneg had to maintain his fulltime job but fortunately his wife was able to cut her work hours to part-time and spend many more days at the hospital. They were not fond of going back and forth, but they were grateful for the accommodations at the long-term housing facility. It was their home away from home.

During one of the trips to H.E.A.R.T., Kenny's dad started thinking about Kenny's reaction to having a sibling. He turned to his wife and spoke in a soft tone, "I know I was the one who resisted having more children." He paused for a moment as he continued to stare at the open road. "I was selfish. I was not thinking about you or Kenny. But the two of you are all I think about now...and I couldn't be happier that Kenny is going to be a big brother." Dorothy Haneg smiled without turning to look at her husband. She didn't need to respond. Her family was back in sync.

Kenny played the "Be Carlos for a Day" game throughout the next day. While his parents sat in his room, he got to try it out on them. Every time he remembered to "Be Carlos", he started experiencing powerful feelings of gratitude for them. He silently introduced Carlos to each of them and he imagined all four of them sitting in his room together. It was a pleasant experience. Even though there were many times throughout the day that he forgot he was playing the game, he kept picking it up again. At the end of the day, he thought about it and he liked the results. He felt like he'd shown Carlos around and that Carlos had witnessed many of the conversations Kenny had with other people. Some of those conversations were with patients who were struggling both physically and emotionally.

"What did you think of our game today?" asked Kenny before he went to sleep that night. "It was nice to be able to talk to my parents with you by my side. But I told you it gets challenging sometimes communicating with some of the other patients."

"I'm glad you paid attention to me while you were also conversing with them," Carlos replied. "But I didn't experience the same frustration that you did."

"How could you not? What did you experience?"

"I felt compassion for them. You were aware of me by your side but they didn't have that same experience. They were going through their day without the awareness of their own eternal being."

"I get it," said Kenny as he felt a rush of adrenalin. "There were many times throughout the day where I forgot about you too and I started to feel down. Then I remembered you and it made me happy. I bet that made you happy too."

"It sure did. Why do you think I really like to play this game?" asked Carlos.

"Because you have a big ego and it's all about you?" Kenny kidded him.

"Very funny. I'm glad you're still not lacking a sense of humor."

Kenny dropped the sarcasm. "Seriously, why do you like to play this game?"

"Repetition."

"Repetition?" repeated Kenny.

"Yes. The more you do something, the more familiar it becomes to you. The more familiar something becomes to you, the more you do it. The result is that you and me end up communicating all day…every day. That is how we become one: repetition. To play the game, we must communicate, you and I. In other words, we must be in communion. If we are in communion…we must already be in union. That means we are now one."

"I like it," said Kenny. "Let's keep playing this game."

✤ ✤ ✤

Over the course of the next few weeks, Kenny and Carlos played the game off and on. Kenny would have liked to have played it more often but he still had the challenge of having his attention constantly pulled away by treatments and the recovery process. One day, it was particularly infrequent that they played the game and Carlos brought it up during their evening conversation.

"Do you still like playing our game?" Carlos asked.

"Yes, I do," acknowledged Kenny. "I'm trying to play as much as I can during the day but I still keep forgetting about you. I want to be you but I guess I'm just not very good at it."

"Sure, you are. Think of what I told you when we came here: you must be aware of our breath and feel my love. You are just not programmed to be me so we need to change the program. Of course, it will take a lot of repetition."

"How do we do that? It's like I need a reminder to play the game that reminds me to think of you."

"Posture," replied Carlos.

"Posture?" Kenny repeated.

"Yes," confirmed Carlos. "Focus on perfect posture."

"I understand why I should be aware of my breath … and to feel only love. But why perfect posture?"

"Your body is like an antenna," Carlos explained. "If you are hunched over, you can't get clear reception to hear me. If you stand up tall, it will be another reminder that we are always in sync."

"Reminders are good, but it still doesn't help if I forget to remind myself."

"If you keep focusing on your posture, you won't be able to forget me."

The next day, Kenny had to go through some treatments. His body felt especially drained from this experience and he was understandably melancholy. Later that night, he kept trying to tune into the feeling of love in order to reach Carlos but it was to no avail. Finally, he thought of his body as a great big antenna and he started to use it to send and receive messages to Carlos. He felt his body naturally start to straighten up. His whole body started to tingle. He saw flashes of light and felt indescribable waves of joy flowing through his body.

"This is it!" he exclaimed.

"Now you're getting it," responded Carlos.

"You're here!"

"Of course, I am here."

"I figured it out," Kenny stated with excitement in his voice. "When I straighten up, I'm like an antenna, or a tuning fork, and my frequency is 'Love'. I feel it. That's how I know I'm in tune with you."

"I couldn't have said it better myself."

"How does it actually work?"

"Each cell in your body is a transmitter, constantly sending and receiving signals. You can sit back and let your cells receive signals from the outside world and send these signals to the rest of the cells in your body, but they may not make you feel very good because they are other people's signals that you are picking up. The alternative is to receive signals from your own image of who you are, which is me, and those will be the signals that are broadcast to the rest of the cells in your body."

Kenny nodded. "I'll tune into your signal."

⚜    ⚜    ⚜

It didn't take long before nurses and staff were commenting on how good Kenny looked. At first, he didn't understand why. Then he realized he was focusing on his posture more and more. He pictured himself like an antenna and it immediately straightened him up. From there, it was much easier to observe his breath. The more he observed his breath, the better he felt because it took his mind off of the daily stresses of *H.E.A.R.T.* It also helped him become more aware of Carlos. He would find himself thinking about Carlos more frequently throughout the day and that triggered more questions in his mind for which he would want to seek answers.

One morning, Kenny was back in his black chair looking at the landscape outside his window. A small gray footstool was positioned in front of the chair and his feet were firmly planted on it. He sat wondering what it must have been like to watch Gaia's first plants grow. Then he started thinking about the first human beings on Gaia. He turned his attention to Carlos for a little help.

"I'm still having trouble understanding where we came from and who created this world."

"You are creating the world you see," Carlos replied.

It was not the response Kenny had been expecting. "I'm creating it? I thought I was more like the creation."

"You are."

"How can I be both the creator and the creation?"

Carlos knew this was an important topic so he took a step back. "Before I came into your body, I was a part of the energy that makes up *All There Is*. As soon as I thought of something, it happened. There was no time lag in the *Field*. So, you can say I was a creator. When I came into your body, we became dependent upon the physical laws of time and space. Because your thoughts don't instantly manifest into physical reality, you don't associate yourself with causing everything to happen around you. Instead, it seems like what happens to you is the effect of everything else. Or in other words, it seems like you are the creation."

"Because I *am* the creation," Kenny corrected.

Carlos continued as if he had not heard Kenny's reply. "We create together, you and I. In the *Field*, I was always able to translate my thoughts instantly into my reality. I was really good at it, too. It was a lot of fun. Here on Gaia, it's the same concept but the process is a little slower. Otherwise, you would be constantly creating things you really didn't want. But if you can imagine it, you can create it. We just need to work together for you to allow it. By yourself, you will always feel like the creation ... and struggle to create your desires. Joining with me, we can co-create whatever you imagine to be true."

"I would like to imagine myself to be healthy."

"Then that is what you should do," said Carlos.

"How am I supposed to just imagine myself to be better?"

"Pretend that is your reality."

"Pretend?"

"Do you remember when you were young and you pretended to be a lion?" Carlos asked.

"Yeah. That was fun."

"Can you pretend to be anything you want?"

"Of course. But it is only pretending."

"If you pretend things to be true, is it a "make-believe" world you are living in?"

"Yeah."

"What is a "make-believe" world? Is it a world where you believe you can make anything happen?"

"I guess."

"Then why not live in that world?"

"Because everyone knows that is not real," Kenny replied curtly.

Carlos was undeterred. "People say that if you pretend something to be true, it's not real. It is just in your imagination. But everything that is real was once imagined. Everything that has already manifested started in someone's imagination. So when people say that when you pretend something, it is not real, they are really saying that when you pretend something, it has not manifested yet, and only things that have manifested are real. But that is not true."

"Why not?"

"If you plant a seed, and you know the plant is coming, is it a 'pretend plant'? Is it 'not real' because you can't see it yet, or does it become real as soon as you plant the seed?"

Kenny thought about this. "I guess it's real when you plant the seed."

"If you pretend to be happy and healthy … are those things real for you as soon as you pretend them to be so, like when you planted the seed and knew it was real even before the plant sprouted out of the ground? Or do you need to wait for something to manifest in the physical world before you can be happy or healthy?"

"I don't think so," Kenny responded with a lack of conviction.

"Kenny, make your beliefs come true by living in a make-believe world. You live in a make-believe world by pretending your dreams have already come true. To pretend is to imagine, and a 'make-believe' world is where you use your imagination and 'make' all your 'beliefs' come true."

"Okay. I can pretend to be healthy, but that doesn't mean it is going to come true."

"For now, don't worry about whether it comes true or not. Just keep pretending you're well."

Kenny thought it was silly but he went to sleep that night pretending that he was cured.

# CHAPTER 6
## THE REFLECTION IN THE MIRROR

Kenny looked in the mirror and stared at the red shirt and blue jeans that was reflecting back at him. It was fitting clothes for his final day at H.E.A.R.T. – comfortable, relaxed and unassuming. His recovery was nothing short of miraculous, they told him. He expected no less. Now it was time to say goodbye to some of the patients and his favorite doctors at the hospital. His feeling of gratitude for being cured was overwhelming.

When it was time, he walked out the front door of H.E.A.R.T. and was met with an overcast sky littered with clouds. As he looked up to the heavens, the sun broke out and shone down upon his face. A smile slowly emerged from the corners of his mouth as euphoric adrenalin swept through his body. Suddenly, a pinch on his forearm startled him and his eyes opened. A brown-haired nurse with her hair pulled back in a tight bun looked down at him and said, "It's time to check your vitals."

Kenny struggled to make sense of what was transpiring. "Was that a dream?' he asked the nurse.

"It must have been," she replied. "You were sleeping like a rock. I'm sorry I had to disturb you."

Kenny didn't respond. When the nurse was finished, he rolled over and went back to sleep.

When he woke up in the morning, he immediately remembered being healthy and walking out the front door of *H.E.A.R.T.* while wearing a red shirt and jeans. He was confused.

"Are you there?" he asked as he looked within for answers.

"Of course, I'm here," Carlos replied.

"That was all a dream last night?"

"Yes, it was," Carlos confirmed.

"But it felt so real!"

"I'm sure it did."

Kenny sat in silence for a while thinking about the dream. His curiosity was getting the better of him. "You said that if I could imagine it, or pretend it was true, it could be real."

"That is true."

"So how does that work? How do you make a dream become a reality?" Kenny asked.

"When you imagine something, you are creating a potential probability in the *Field*. When you start to feel as if it is true, the *Field* reflects it back to you so you can experience it."

"What do you mean it 'reflects it back to me'?"

"Let's look at it another way. When you look in the mirror, what do you see?"

"I see my reflection," replied Kenny.

"Does the mirror always reflect back exactly what is shown to it, or does the mirror change it?"

"No, the mirror doesn't change it. I guess it reflects back exactly what is shown to it. If I raise two fingers into the mirror, it always reflects back two fingers."

"Exactly. Does it ever make mistakes?"

"No. The mirror can't make mistakes."

"Is it safe to say that the mirror is perfect?"

"Yes, you can say that. It's perfect," Kenny confirmed.

"And how do you change what you see in the mirror?"

"You change what you show it."

"Very good," said Carlos. "Now, what if I told you that the entire *Field* is a mirror?"

"Are you saying the *Field* is a mirror that reflects back to me in Gaia?" asked Kenny.

"Yes."

"Well, that doesn't always seem to work."

"Are you saying that sometimes you experience things you didn't project into the mirror?"

"Exactly."

"But the mirror never makes mistakes," Carlos reminded him. "You said it yourself."

"I thought you said that," Kenny replied.

"No, it was you," corrected Carlos.

Kenny threw his hands up in the air. "Whatever."

Carlos could sense Kenny was losing interest and he did not want to let go of this conversation. "I have explained this differently to you in the past, but it still works the same. When you imagine something and feel as if it has already come true, you are sending vibrations or signals into the *Field*, which acts like a giant mirror that reflects those images directly back to you so you can experience them. The *Field*, or the *Giant Mirror*, doesn't change anything. The only things that ever change are the images you send to the *Field*."

Kenny wasn't buying it. "I want to be healthy but I'm still sick. Why isn't this giant mirror of yours reflecting back health?"

"Therein lies your dilemma," said Carlos. "You want to be healthy but you don't fully believe it to be true. When you fully believe that you are well, and not sick, that is what will be reflected back to you."

"You know I want to be healthy!" exclaimed Kenny as he felt his frustration rise. "Why can't you just make me healthy?"

"I reflect back to you who you are being."

"Yes, I get that!" Kenny exclaimed. "But if you are me, why can't you change first?"

"Kenny, stand in front of the mirror," Carlos directed. Kenny did as he was instructed.

"Now look at your body... and then look at your reflection in the mirror. Which moves first?"

Kenny stared at himself in the mirror for a minute. "I guess my body moves first."

"Keep watching for a little while," said Carlos. "Does the reflection always do what the body does?"

"Yes."

"Does the reflection in the mirror ever move first and then your body follows?"

"No, of course not."

"Well, if you want to change your reflection, why would you ever expect it to move first?"

Kenny froze. *Am I creating the reflection?* he thought to himself. *I didn't choose to be in this hospital.* He turned his attention back to Carlos. "All I know is that I'm sick, and you expect me to believe that I'm somehow responsible for that? That my life is being reflected back to me because this is what I want? Are you kidding?"

"It's more than that, Kenny. Your life is not just being reflected back to you. Your life *is* the reflection."

Later that evening, Kenny found himself looking into the mirror again. He started to imagine that he was Carlos and Carlos was looking back at him. As he studied his reflection, Kenny asked the reflection in the mirror, "Is that you, or is this me I'm looking at?"

"This is us," answered Carlos from the reflection in the mirror.

A smile slowly consumed Kenny's face.

"So, I can be Kenny... or I can be Carlos. Is that what you're saying?"

"That's right," said Carlos. "And whoever you are being right now, that is who is being reflected back to you from the *Field*. It becomes like a feedback loop. The longer you can be aware of being me, the longer the *Field* keeps reflecting that back to you, which reinforces you being me... and it keeps expanding from there."

An impulse suddenly came to Kenny. He quickly walked into his room and grabbed a black magic marker from his desk and took it back to the bathroom mirror. As he stared at the reflection looking back at him, he reached up and wrote three words across the top of the mirror:

**This Is Us!**

The next morning, Kenny walked into the bathroom and saw what he'd scribbled onto the mirror the night before. He looked directly into the mirror and tried not to focus on the guy with the bald head and sleepy eyes staring back at him.

"This is us, isn't it?" he asked.

"Yes, it is," answered Carlos from the reflection in the mirror. "From now on, when you look into the mirror, the question will always be: 'Who do you see?' If you can only see yourself, you won't be able to recognize that I am right here with you. That is me in the mirror, and I am always reflecting back to you exactly who you are in this moment. That is also what you are experiencing in your life. So, you can change the reflection and change your life, by changing who you are being, because the mirror is just a reflection of who you are being right now. It is a reflection of your consciousness."

"But my life is influenced by other people too," said Kenny. "I can't control what they say or do, and yet they clearly have an influence on the world I see."

"The world you see is just a shadow," responded Carlos.

"A shadow of what?"

"A shadow of who you are all being right now. It is a shadow of your collective consciousness."

"Okay. If that's true … then I have only one more question for you."

"What's that?"

"If I don't like what I see, how do I change the reflection? And if collectively, we don't like what we see, how do we change the shadow? How do we change who we're being?"

"Congratulations," said Carlos.

"For what?"

"You just asked the most fundamental question of reality."

Kenny wasn't satisfied. "That's great... but what's the answer?"

"The answer is not so simple."

"You're kidding, right? Just try me ...".

"Very well," Carlos started. "Your consciousness is an individualized piece of all consciousness. And although you are not a separate individual from the whole, your 'individualized' consciousness had to start somewhere. So, let's start with something you may be familiar with."

"What's that?"

"The Big Bang."

"I've heard of that," Kenny said with renewed excitement. "That's where everything on Gaia started."

"That's right. Before the Big Bang, your physical reality did not exist. After the Big Bang, nothing became something. The something was particles or pixels. And these particles or pixels were in the form of matter, but were still contained within the one consciousness. They were just a different form of energy or consciousness. You call that physical form. So no-thing became some-thing, which together made up every-thing."

Carlos paused, and Kenny said, "Go on."

"You keep looking at the evolution of your planet and you think that's where time began. But we must first start with the evolution of the particles of the Big Bang. They did not start in your physical 3-D reality. Before Gaia was born, these were particles in a higher dimension which projected out a version of itself into a lower dimension. Then, that new version of consciousness projected itself out again to create the 3-D version of the world you see. Is it the exact same as the original particles from the Big Bang? Yes and no."

Kenny frowned. "What does that mean?"

"All life forms that you are aware of are a finite version of the infinite. That means they came from the original consciousness and will return to the original consciousness. And while they are here, they are either experiencing the awareness of that consciousness ... or they are experiencing the absence of awareness of that consciousness. Some life forms on Gaia are always aware of that consciousness. You call that nature. A flower doesn't think about being conscious of what it is. It just is – and it never deviates from being a flower. But humans have been given the choice of who they want to be. You call that free will. That is why you have the choice to be me or not to be me."

"I get it. My choice is that I am you or I am not you."

"Precisely."

"That's all nice and dandy, but you still didn't answer my question."

"Which is?"

Kenny asked again, "How do I change who I am being? I know that I want to be aware of being you. But if I find myself not being aware of you, or not being who I would like to be, how do I change who I am being in that moment? How do I change who I am being so I can change my reflection from being not healthy to being healthy?"

"I am healthy, Kenny. And if you are me, then you must be healthy too."

"In case you were wondering, it's not that easy to just be you!"

"I am your imagination. So, if you are me, you are just being who you imagine yourself to be. That means that if you want to be healthy, you must imagine yourself as being healthy, and that is who we become."

"I just think about being healthy and then it happens?"

"Not quite," said Carlos.

"I knew it wasn't that easy!"

"That was just incomplete. You not only think about it, but you must imagine what it would *feel* like to be healthy. Who you are being is not just about what you are thinking. It is a projection of how you are feeling. So how you are feeling creates the projection of who you are being... which in turn creates the reflection that you experience. That experience is called your life."

"I think I'm really beginning to understand this," said Kenny sincerely. "Thank you for this understanding mind."

❧ ❧ ❧

For the next few days, Kenny couldn't stop thinking about the reflection and the shadow. He kept trying to remember how Carlos had explained them. The more he thought about it, the more confused he got. He knew he had to go back to the source for more clarity. The following morning, he reached out to Carlos again.

"I have to take back what I said before. I don't think I have such an understanding mind anymore."

"Kenny, an understanding mind is a wonderful thing to have. But there is more to understanding than that."

"What could be more important than that?"

"You need to create coherence between your brain and your heart. To truly have an understanding mind, you must first have an understanding heart."

Kenny was quiet, then said, "Let me think about that for a minute."

"Stop thinking about me. Just feel me."

"Don't you think I'm *trying* to feel you?" said Kenny. "Sometimes you get buried in all my thoughts and I have to find you first."

"I am not in your head. I am in your heart," Carlos clarified.

"But I can't get my thoughts out of my head and into my heart."

"Sure, you can."

"Yeah … if I could put my heart in my brain."

"You don't have to. Just use your *Heart Brain*," said Carlos.

"Very funny."

"I'm serious."

"What are you talking about?" Kenny replied skeptically.

"Your heart has similar characteristics to the brain in your head. So the more you access the feeling in your heart, the more you activate your *Heart Brain*."

Kenny raised an eyebrow. "You're telling me I have two brains: one in my head and one in my heart?"

"You could say that – and the one in your heart is the one you should focus on."

"How can I focus on it if I never knew it existed?"

"Well now you do, so you have no excuse anymore not to focus on it."

"And just how do I do that?" Kenny asked.

"A good place to start is by placing your hand over your heart and feeling it. Feel your heart beat while you are focusing on your breath. Put your heart in charge of everything. Your heart's brain will take over from there. It doesn't listen to what other people say. It doesn't judge what other people do. It doesn't worry about what might happen. It only knows right now. It only feels love and compassion. If you feel good inside, you know your *Heart Brain* is in charge."

"Is that all?"

"No, there's more."

"I was only kidding," said Kenny.

"I'm not," replied Carlos. "An understanding mind allows you to know more. An understanding heart allows you to feel more. When you are aware of your *Heart Brain*, you feel it. You envelop it. You let it completely control your physical body. So put your intentions in your *Heart Brain*. That is the image you want to feel. That is the reflection you want to see in the mirror. Feel the joy of experiencing those images in your heart."

Carlos continued. "Once you can feel the joy of experiencing your intentions in your heart, then they have already been created. They have already happened in the *Field*. Now it is just a matter of converting those images from your vibrational reality to your physical reality. Since feeling is the language of the subconscious mind and how you communicate with the *Field*, then as long as you focus on the feeling of your intentions coming true, they must transform from vibrational images in the *Field* to material images in the Land of Perception and Time."

"I only have one intention," Kenny said firmly.

"What is that?"

"I want to walk out the front door of *H.E.A.R.T.* completely healed."

"Then place that intention in your *Heart Brain*."

Kenny went over to his desk and sat down. He pulled out a pad of paper and proceeded to draw a picture of himself walking out the front door. He picked it up and held it to his *Heart Brain*. The feeling was electric. He was overcome with joy and appreciation of that image as he let himself fall back onto his chair.

# CHAPTER 7
# THE PUPIL BECOMES THE TEACHER

Kenny wanted to start to tell some of the other patients about Carlos, especially James. During their lunch hour was when he spoke with them most frequently, so he decided that was the best time and place to bring it up. He walked into the Community Room and saw James talking with Danny in the far corner of the room. Danny was the tallest patient in Kenny's wing of the hospital. He appeared even taller than he was because his posture was impeccable. When he stood up, he lifted his chin to the sky and his tall, thin frame pointed up like a radio antenna. He also talked more quickly than most other patients while exuding a nervous energy at all times. Kenny headed over to the corner and sat down on a bright-colored sofa facing the two of them. As soon as he was seated, he heard a voice from the doorway saying, "Hey guys, I thought I would find you here."

Stevie walked in with her trademark bandana on her head and a grin from ear to ear. Kenny smiled at how uplifting Stevie always seemed to be no matter what she was going through. Stevie was the most positive person he had ever met. While they engaged in small talk, Kenny thought about how he would explain his communication with Carlos to his closest friends at *H.E.A.R.T.* This was as good a time as there ever would be, so after some trepidation, he finally spoke up:

"Do you ever think about how we got here?"

The trio turned to him with confused looks on their faces.

"What do you mean?" asked James. 'How we got to *H.E.A.R.T.*?"

Kenny shook his head. "You know, where we came from?"

"Yeah, my mother's belly," Stevie chimed in, and she laughed at her own comment.

Kenny stayed focused. "I mean before that."

James was still unsure where this was going. "You lost me, Kenny."

Kenny paused. *That didn't go so well,* he thought to himself. "Let's change the question. Do you guys ever talk to yourselves at night?"

"Yeah," said Stevie with a grin still on her face. "I always ask myself questions and I always get all the right answers."

"I'm serious." Kenny continued to try to figure out the right approach about sharing his conversations with Carlos. "I don't mean talking to your physical self, but more like talking to your non-physical self."

"Do you mean like talking to your soul?" asked Danny.

"I'm not sure," Kenny responded a little more comfortably. "Maybe more like your 'eternal being', although I don't know how that is different from our soul."

James was growing curious. "Where do we find our eternal being?"

"It's inside of us ... but it comes from the *Field*."

"What field?" asked Danny.

"*The Field of Potential Probabilities.*"

"What kind of field is that?"

"It's a field of energy," Kenny responded confidently.

"And where is this field?"

"The *Field* is everywhere."

Danny was getting skeptical. "So let me get this straight. You talk to this eternal being who says it comes from a field that is everywhere ...."

Kenny started to realize how far-fetched this sounded. Still, he didn't want to back down.

"Yes," he said with as much conviction as he could muster up.

"And what language do they speak in this field?" asked Danny.

"That's where it gets interesting," explained Kenny. "They don't speak words in the *Field*."

"Then how do you hear it?" asked James.

"You don't. You feel it."

As soon as the words left his mouth, Kenny realized they would be hard to comprehend.

"That's ridiculous," Danny shot back. "How do you feel words?"

"Look," said Kenny very calmly. "I don't know how else to explain this. I don't talk to it with words. We communicate through my thoughts and feelings."

Immediately everyone started talking at once. Kenny could feel frustration start to sink in. This was not how he expected this conversation to go...but he never completely thought it out ahead of time either.

"Guys, listen!" Kenny shouted in desperation. "Think about it. We all come from somewhere before we're born. Agreed?"

"Well...yeah," Danny muttered.

"Well, where is that?" Kenny continued. "Where do you think we come from?"

There were no responses.

"Since you don't have any better explanations, let's just assume we come from this *Field of Energy*. And if it's real...then we all have access to it."

James nodded. "Okay. Suppose there is a Field that we all came from. How does that change anything?"

Kenny looked at James with renewed excitement. "That changes everything. If we all come from a Field of Energy...and we are still connected to that *Field* now...then we can start to change our lives here in Gaia."

"And just how do we do that?" James asked.

"By how we think and how we feel. That is how we connect to the *Field*...and when we do...we can change our energy."

Kenny was interrupted by the sound of a chair sliding along the floor. The four boys turned their heads and saw an intern with long blonde hair and a white jacket standing up from a nearby table. None of them had noticed her earlier. They watched as she quietly left the room.

Stevie was having trouble processing all this information about fields and energy. "Can we finish this tomorrow?" she asked.

"That's a good idea," said Danny as he stood up and followed the intern out the door.

Later that night, Kenny thought about the conversation with his friends and started to share it with Carlos.

"I tried to talk to some of the guys about you today but it didn't go so well."

Carlos had a different view on the discussion. "It went just fine," he countered.

"How can you say that? They looked at me like I had two heads."

"Did you expect them to fully understand what the *Field* is the first time they heard about it?"

"Well, not really," Kenny admitted.

Carlos knew that Kenny needed some more reassurance. "You had to start somewhere and you planted the first seed with them. If your intention is ultimately to help them … then stay the course and that seed will grow within them."

Kenny flashed a determined smile. "Okay. That's what I'll do."

It didn't take long for the seed to grow. Kenny went very slowly at first and tried to simplify some of Carlos's messages. Each night, Kenny and a few of his friends would sit around Kenny's bed and he would share more stories about Carlos and what he had learned from him. It started to bring them great comfort and slowly his audience grew. Soon they were meeting back in the Community Room for a few evenings each week.

One evening after a particularly positive talk with his friends, he couldn't wait to share his joy with Carlos.

"New guys are coming each week and I haven't even had to invite them."

Carlos reinforced his enthusiasm. "You changed your consciousness. Now, your willingness to help others is all you need. They will keep finding you."

"I'm willing to help them if I can, but what if I can't? What if I run out of things to talk about?"

"Maybe you're supposed to show the other patients how to connect to their own eternal being."

Kenny shook his head. "You're the teacher. Not me."

"So how do you connect to me?" Carlos asked.

"I don't know. I just do it."

"Explain it to me."

"Well, when I'm not in a good mood, I can never seem to reach you."

"That's good. Keep going."

"At night it's easier than during the day. But as you know, as soon as I wake up in the morning is the best time for us to talk. The earlier the better. If I didn't know better, I'd think you were sitting around and waiting for me to wake up in the morning."

"Of course, I am," confirmed Carlos. "I can't wait to be in your body again. But how do you specifically connect to me?"

"Well, I try to do what you said you came here to do. First, I get comfortable in a chair. Then I sit up and pull my shoulder blades back for good posture. Then I start thinking about how my breath moves through my body. Once I become fully aware of my breath, I start to feel it move from my butt all the way to the top of my head. Then I think about how much you love being in my body. Now that I've been doing this long enough, I know you will always come and

I'm really appreciative of that. Once I start communicating with you, I feel like you're vibrating inside of me."

Carlos was pleased. "That's a beautiful thing."

"Wait! What are you asking me for?" said Kenny. "You know what I do."

"Yes, I do. But if I can get you to describe it to me, like you just did, it makes it clearer for you as to what you're doing ... and then you can describe it to others."

"Very sneaky."

"I prefer to think of it as very clever."

⚜ ⚜ ⚜

The other young patients grew excited about Kenny's stories. Kenny had them use their imaginations and pretend they were all from this *Field of Potential Probabilities*. One afternoon, he created a chant which he continued to repeat as often as he could.

"Where are we from?" he yelled out loud.

"The *Field*!" everyone answered in unison.

Kenny surveyed the room. He could feel the energy level of the room rise as each of his friends began to imagine themselves in a field of energy. Their thoughts had transformed them from the hospital surroundings to their own imaginary place. The staff at the hospital were aware of what was going on but they didn't seem to find any harm in it.

As Kenny and some of the patients continued to sit in the Community Room, Danny asked, "Do you really think we can get healthy again?"

"My intention is not to 'get' healthy," replied Kenny. "My intention is to feel as if I am already healthy."

"What's the difference?" Danny asked.

"If my intention is to 'get' healthy, it may or may not happen because I might start to doubt it, and then it can't happen. But if I feel as if I am already healthy, then it has a much better chance of happening."

"But it hasn't happened yet," said Danny.

"That depends on how you look at time."

"What do you mean?"

Kenny thought about the concept of time as he understood it from Carlos. He tried to picture in his mind how he would explain it to them and images slowly started to appear in his mind. He stood up and went over to the whiteboard that nurses used for messages to the patients. He erased what was on the board and then he picked up a magic marker and began to draw.

"This is just an image of linear time as we know it on Gaia," he explained to the others. "It goes on forever."

"Okay," said Danny.

Kenny continued to draw. "This is what it was like when Carlos was watching the formation of Gaia. Dust and gases formed a solid crust of rock and then plants and living organisms started to grow."

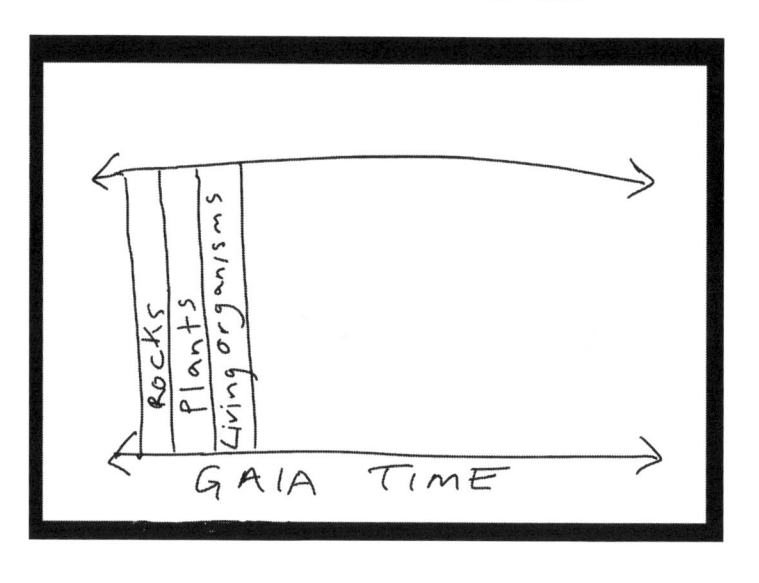

"That's pretty cool," said Stevie. "You better watch out. People will start calling you 'Kenny the Whiteboard Guy'." The others chuckled at Kenny's new nickname.

Next, Kenny explained how eternal beings started to get assigned to Gaia so they could experience themselves in a physical body. He drew a few dashes on the paper and then explained the concept of a dash, which just signified the time that each human spent on Gaia.

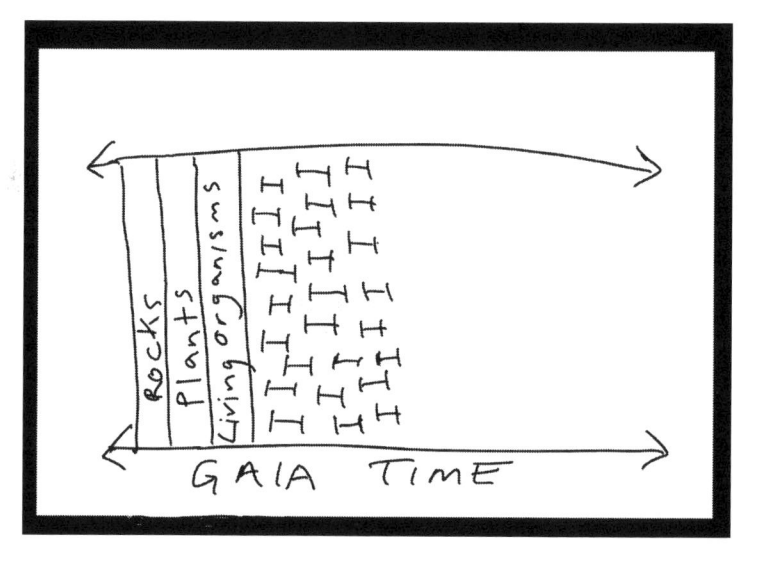

Finally, Kenny explained the concept of NOW, and how everyone living on Gaia right now was participating in their dash. He showed them how some dashes last longer than others, but that they all eventually end. He also showed them how it is always NOW.

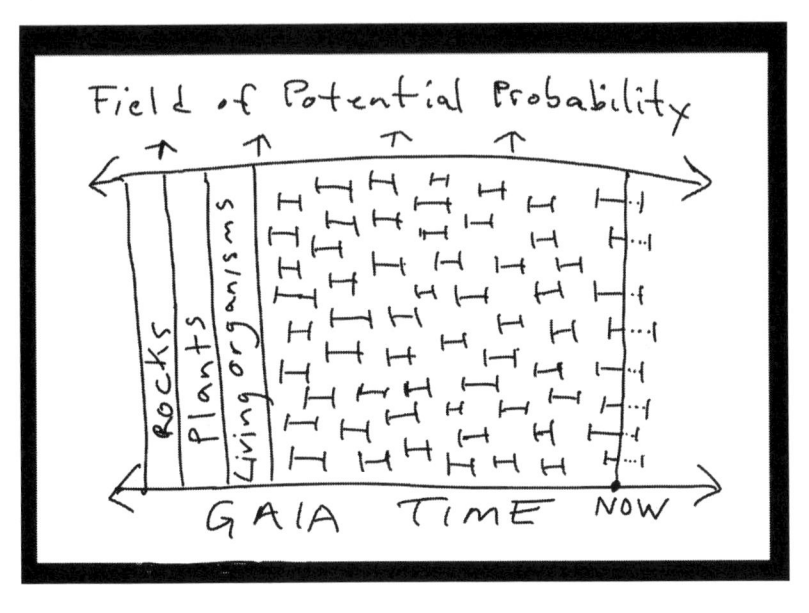

James studied the last picture that Kenny drew. He was fixated on NOW. "What about the future?" he asked. "How do we get there?"

"You can't physically go there," Kenny explained. "Just like you can't physically go back to the past. But you *can* go to the past or the future with your thoughts. When you think about the past or the future, you can mix those thoughts with love or fear and that determines how we feel. Carlos says we're always looking at the past or future through the Lens of Love or the Lens of Fear, and that's our perception. Since it is always NOW, he said that time is just a measurement we use to differentiate between our perception of reality."

"What kind of reality is that?" asked Danny.

"It's the one we've created based on our thoughts and emotions."

"But how do we know which lens we are using?" asked James.

"How you feel inside will always tell you which lens you're looking through."

"But again, what about the future?" asked James. "How do we look at that with love when we don't know what's going to happen?"

"That's the best part. Whichever lens you look at the future with determines what's going to happen for you."

James stared at the pictures, surrounded by others wearing matching blank faces. There were no more questions after that.

⚜ ⚜ ⚜

Later that night, Kenny told Carlos all about the conversation that he'd had that afternoon regarding time. Everyone had been fascinated with what he had to say and they'd asked great questions. But as Kenny had been answering those questions, it had sparked new ones that he wasn't sure about.

"Can I ask you something else about time?"

"Of course," said Carlos.

"You said we're not the only *Land of Perception and Time*."

"That's right."

"And that we're all connected to the same source energy."

"That is correct."

"So does that mean that I can communicate with other *Lands of Perception and Time?*"

"Yes," said Carlos, "but not in the way that you think. Let's look at it this way. Every thought you have ever had is stored in the *Field of Potential Probabilities*. That is the same with every human-like species in every *Land of Perception and Time*. So, do you have access to thoughts from other *Lands?* Yes. But can you directly communicate with beings in other *Lands* from your position here on Gaia? No. And why would you want to? What they are actually experiencing is unique to them, just like what you are experiencing on Gaia is unique to everyone who comes to this particular *Land of Perception and Time*."

"So, I really can't communicate with other *Lands*?"

"You can access information from other *Lands*."

Kenny shrugged. "How do I do that?"

"You tap into the frequency of the *Field*."

"How do I know if I'm tapping into the right *Field*? What if that *Land* has a different *Field* and therefore a different frequency?"

"There are many *Lands* but only one *Field*. All the information from every one of the *Lands* is fed into the same *Field*. Tune into that *Field* and you can access information from any *Land*."

Kenny went to sleep trying to imagine how there could be many *Lands* contained in only one *Field*.

⚜ ⚜ ⚜

The next day, Kenny was waiting to go to lunch when James walked by his room. James popped his head in, glanced into Kenny's bathroom, and noticed something written on his mirror.

"What's that?" he asked as he motioned his head towards the bathroom.

"What's what?" Kenny asked.

"What's written on your mirror?"

Kenny realized what he was referring to and he immediately jumped up to go erase what was on the mirror. It was too late. James was already reading it.

"*This Is Us*," he read aloud. "What does that mean?"

Kenny explained the concept of the mirror and how it related to the *Field*. "The mirror helps me understand how everything is reflected back to me," he concluded, "especially the image of Carlos."

James was intrigued. "Are you saying that when you look in the mirror you see Carlos?"

"Yes. I see both of us," said Kenny. "But do me a favor. I'm not ready to share this with anyone yet. Okay?"

James reassured him. "Yeah, sure. No problem. We'll keep it between the two of us."

But as soon as they got to the lunch table, James couldn't control himself. He immediately told the other patients about the note written on Kenny's mirror. Kenny kept looking at James in disbelief that he would share his secret, but James avoided his stare. It was too late anyway.

"Oh yeah! I always see someone else staring back at me when I look in the mirror," said Danny sarcastically.

"What color hair does Carlos have?" asked Stevie.

"What are you talking about? It's me!" said Kenny. Frustration started to fill his body. "Carlos looks like me, okay?"

Stevie was still curious. "Then how do you know it's him?"

"I feel him," said Kenny. "I don't know how else to describe it."

Stevie wasn't finished yet. "Can I come to your room and see him?"

"What?"

"Can I come to your room and look at Carlos in your mirror?"

"You don't need to do that," said Kenny. "Go look into your own mirror."

Stevie was still confused. "You mean Carlos is in my mirror too?"

"No!" shouted Kenny. "YOUR eternal being is in YOUR mirror."

"You mean I have an eternal being too?"

"Everyone has an eternal being and you are always connected to it," said Kenny, beginning to calm down.

James stepped in. "You're saying that we can talk to our eternal being the same way you talk to Carlos?"

"Of course, you can," said Kenny. "Just because you haven't done it yet, doesn't mean you can't. Start small. Just ask over and over for an understanding mind. That's something you already crave deep within you. Better yet, just make a game out of it."

"What kind of game?" asked James.

"I don't know. You can call it ...'Who's my Carlos?'"

"How do you play?"

"Keep saying over and over, 'Who's my Carlos? I know you're there.' Then silently wait for answers. If that's your number one priority, to have communication with your eternal being, then it will come. I guarantee it!"

Each of the friends began thinking about the possibility of having their own eternal being. Their minds drifted and it was quiet for the rest of the lunch.

❧ ❧ ❧

James had always found things to be grateful for. But the daily routine and the treatments he was receiving at *H.E.A.R.T.* every day were making it increasingly difficult to be grateful. If there was one exception, it was that he was grateful for his cochlear implants. It was his lifeline to communicating with the other patients and doctors. He had been wearing them for as long as he could remember.

Prior to his first birthday, James's mother started to get very concerned about her son's potential lack of hearing. She noticed that James rarely turned towards her when she talked to him. Loud noises did not seem to have much effect on him either. When she approached her husband to talk about James, he would dismiss her concerns as being premature and overly cautious.

James started to walk shortly after he turned one years old, and his mother's concerns were quickly relieved. Each night, she would hear her husband's car pull into the garage beneath their family room and James would immediately run over to the door to wait for his father to come up the stairs and greet him. Perhaps her husband was right, she thought. James could hear just fine. She was just being an overly cautious mom.

Unfortunately, that comfort didn't last long. A mother's intuition is rarely proved false. Despite the possibility that he could hear his father's car when he arrived home at night, there were a growing number of instances when it seemed like his hearing was impaired. Otherwise, there could be other serious issues confronting James. One afternoon, his mother took him to a hearing specialist and was floored by the analysis. James was profoundly deaf.

That night, she sat down with her husband and discussed James' condition. They were searching for reasons for how it could be.

"But he always heard your car every night," she said with a sense of desperation.

Her husband took a long pause before answering, "Maybe he didn't hear my car. The garage is under the family room. He must have just felt the vibrations."

There was another pause.

"I guess you're right," she replied.

From that point on, the research was swift and the conclusion was clear. By the time he reached eighteen months old, James was fitted for cochlear implants. He was attending pre-school at four years old and the other kids barely noticed the small processors behind his ears that allowed him to interpret sound vibrations into coherent words.

Despite his hearing impairment, James continued to be a happy boy. He loved the outdoors and spent as much time as he could outside the house. He enjoyed tending to his mother's garden. In the spring they would plant his favorite vegetables: lettuce, tomatoes and cucumbers. During autumn, they would reap the harvest. He seemed to have boundless energy in his body and a constant smile on his face. Then things started to change.

Toiling in the garden became a strain on him. He would experience shortness of breath with only minor exertion. When his mother noticed his legs were getting swollen, she quickly took him to a medical specialist. The diagnosis was devastating. James had congestive heart failure. Once again, the research was swift and the conclusion was clear. James was going to one of the top pediatric hospitals in the world. That is what brought him to the *H.E.A.R.T.* facility.

Now he could feel another change taking place. Each day and night, he started to look forward to attending Kenny's sit around. He was intrigued with Kenny's conversations with Carlos. He started playing the game, 'Who's my Carlos?' Over and over, he would ask that question. When he didn't get a response, doubt would set in.

*Do I even* have *an eternal being?* he asked himself rhetorically. *I must. Carlos told Kenny that we all do. I just can't hear mine because I take off my processors when I go to bed at night.*

*Or can I?* he wondered.

He lay back in bed and thought about some of the things Kenny had shared about communicating with his eternal being. He sat up, got comfortable, focused on his breath...and he only thought about things that he really loved. Then he started to ask questions.

"I know you're here. Even though I don't have my implants in, I don't believe that can stop me from hearing you. If you're really here, can you give me some kind of a sign? That would help me a lot."

James kept talking but got no response. Just before he nodded off to sleep, he reached for a glass of water on his bedside table. As he did, the magazine that was on the edge of his nightstand fell onto the floor. He leaned down to pick it up and he noticed it was open to the page on horoscopes. At the top of the page was the horoscope for Leo. He looked at it and read the message that accompanied it:

> **There are no coincidences. They are synchron-icities waiting for your recognition.**

James stared at the horoscope.

"Your name is Leo, isn't it," he said out loud to no one in particular.

"Yes, it is," Leo replied without expecting a response.

"I knew it!" James exclaimed.

"What?" Leo shouted out in surprise. He was stunned that he was actually communicating with his human self.

"I knew I had an eternal being...and now I know your name," said James.

"*Our* name," corrected Leo.

"Yes, 'our' name," agreed James.

They communicated with each other for hours. James asked question after question, similar to Kenny quizzing Carlos about everything he could think of. Leo was ecstatic that he could finally share his wisdom with his human self.

"Wait!" said James.

"What is it?"

"I just realized I took off my processor before going to bed. If I can't hear you, how are we having this conversation?"

"I was waiting for you to ask that question," said Leo.

"Can you explain it to me?" replied James.

"In order to hear in the physical world, you must interpret sound vibrations with your ears. It's not too difficult because the speed of sound is slower than the speed of light. Just as you can't interpret sound vibrations without your implants, human ears can't interpret vibrations beyond your physical reality. You have to tune into a different frequency to interpret the vibrations coming from the *Field*. That's because the vibrations from the Field are faster than the speed of light. The physical senses you have grown accustomed to using won't work for you in this new realm. You have to go beyond your physical senses."

"I always thought it was so important to be able to hear other people," said James. "Now you're saying there's much more than that?"

"I know it has always meant a lot to you to be able to communicate with other people," said Leo. "But physical communication with other humans is only the beginning. Remember that when you are interpreting vibrations that are coming from other people, they don't always make you feel good. In essence, you are at the effect of the vibrations that are coming from them. But non-physical communication is where the fun starts. That is when you are interpreting vibrations that are faster than the speed of light – and those vibrations are going to make you feel amazing because those vibrations are coming from the *Field*. Those vibrations are coming from where I am. That is how you and I are communicating right now."

James couldn't believe what was happening. He was overcome with joy and appreciation. "Thank you for allowing me to talk with you," he said with deep sincerity.

"Don't thank me," said Leo. "I didn't lower my vibrations to communicate with you, James. You had to raise your vibrations to communicate with me. Every one of you has the potential to do this. Not all of you actually do it."

It wasn't long before James fell into a very deep sleep.

❧ ❧ ❧

The following day, James couldn't stop thinking about his conversation with Leo. When his nurse came into his room to check on his vitals, she noticed a grin on his face.

"You seem happy this morning," she commented.

"Yes I am. Why wouldn't I be," he responded.

"Can't think of a good reason why you wouldn't," she countered as a smile appeared on her face as well.

Later on, James went to lunch and sat with some of the other patients. He couldn't contain his excitement. "Has anyone been playing 'Who's my Carlos?' he asked the group.

"I tried for a little while but I didn't get anywhere," said Stevie.

"I don't know if I even have an eternal being," Danny added reluctantly.

"Why do you ask?" said Kenny.

"Just curious," James replied. "Oh….and also…I know 'my Carlos' is named Leo."

"Yes!" shouted the group in unison. There was an explosion of excitement. James went on to explain his encounter with Leo the night before. Everyone listened with heightened emotions. Their walls of doubt started to come crumbling down. Over the next few weeks more of them would start to connect to their own eternal being.

Kenny was excited for his friend as well but there was something that was puzzling him. He chose not to share it with his friends. He just smiled and congratulated James.

James saw the look on Kenny's face and asked, "Is everything okay, Kenny?"

"Sure," said Kenny with a little hesitation. After a brief pause, he quietly asked, "Do you sleep with your cochlear implants on?"

James smiled and said, "Now I understand what is puzzling you. I don't sleep with my processor on and I wasn't wearing it when I spoke with Leo. But I did ask Leo how I was able to hear him."

James explained to his friends what Leo had told him about vibrations, frequencies and non-physical communication. Danny was especially interested in this conversation because radio frequencies were his hobby.

Kenny couldn't stop thinking about James's conversation with his higher self. He never really thought about how he was communicating with Carlos, but now he was very curious. He couldn't wait to ask Carlos about it.

As soon as he got back to his room, he went straight to his black chair to initiate his dialogue with Carlos. "James said he communicates with his eternal being at night, even without his processor on. Can you believe that?"

"Yes. He does not need hearing implants to communicate with Leo."

"Wait," said Kenny. "How did you know his name was Leo?"

"Leo and I were friends in the *Field*. We both wanted to come to Gaia at the same time. I always imagined what it would be like to meet him in physical form. I didn't know it would be in this hospital."

It was almost too much information for Kenny to process. He paused and stared out the window. "Is that why I always felt a connection to James?" he finally asked.

"Yes. That is one reason why," Carlos replied.

Kenny tried to imagine what it was like to know James before they were born into this *Land of Perception and Time* called Gaia. *How did they communicate before they got here? What brought them to this place? How are they communicating now with their eternal beings?* There were so many unanswered questions.

*One at a time,* Kenny thought to himself. *Just ask one at a time.* He finally turned his attention back to Carlos.

"If James can't hear me, how does he hear Leo?"

"The same way you hear me."

"How do I hear you?"

"You interpret my vibrations."

"How am I doing that?"

"First you need to raise your vibrations, because I don't lower my vibrations to meet you. That's why you focus on our breath and feel my love."

"Yes, I get that. But *how* am I doing it?" Kenny asked emphatically.

"Don't think about 'how' to do it. Just allow yourself to feel our vibrations and trust that you will be able to interpret them."

"What if I can't?"

"Do you think about how you interpret sound vibrations with your ears when someone is talking to you?"

Kenny shrugged. "I guess not."

"You are constantly interpreting the sounds you hear into words that someone is saying. You don't doubt your ability to hear exactly what that person is communicating to you. You trust your ability to translate those vibrations accurately. But when I communicate to you, which I am doing all day long, you don't always trust the process."

"It's easier to hear things that are real, than hear things that aren't real," Kenny stated.

"You mean it's easier to hear things in your physical reality than in your vibrational reality. That is understandable because you have been trained to listen to those sound vibrations in the physical world all of your human life. But there are others who cannot hear sound vibrations in the physical world but can interpret our vibrational frequency quite effortlessly."

"You mean like James?"

"Yes, just like James. He cannot interpret sound vibrations in the physical world but he can hear us just fine. We are just on a different vibrational frequency. It's like a dog whistle. Just because you may not be able to hear it, doesn't mean there is no sound to someone else. Your dog can still hear it."

Kenny smiled. "Isn't it ironic that James may not be able to hear others without his implants, but he can communicate with his inner being any time? At the same time, someone else may be able to communicate with others verbally, but maybe they aren't communicating with their own inner being."

"Yes," agreed Carlos. "Ironic indeed."

"So how do I help them?" asked Kenny. How do I explain to the others that I can communicate with you from Gaia while you're still in the *Field*?"

"Think of it this way," said Carlos. "Whenever you talk to your friends, you are communicating with each other on Gaia and you appear to be separate individuals. When you talk with me, we must be vibrationally joined together as one in order to communicate – or to be in communion – in the *Field*. Therefore, if we are in communion, we are already in union. We must be in union ... because you cannot have comm-union without union.

"You're saying that any time you and I are talking, we have to be connected in the *Field*?"

"Yes."

Kenny thought about this. "That makes sense. But what do you mean that when I'm talking to my friends, we *appear* to be two separate individuals? We *are* separate."

"You are not separate."

"Of course, we are."

"Kenny, we came from the *Field* and we will return to the *Field*. While we are here, the *Field* will reflect back to you exactly who you are being in every moment. Why? Because you are still in the *Field*!"

"How is that possible? I thought I was in the *Land of Perception and Time*."

"You are. The *Land* is within the *Field*. You never left the *Field* because you can't leave the *Field*. The *Field* is all there is. The *Field* goes on for eternity and stretches to infinity. So the *Field* is indivisible, meaning you can't be separate from it and neither can your friends. There is no place that the *Field* ends and you begin. You can't be an individual piece of the *Field* that is separate from it. You are an individualized piece of the whole that is still connected to the *Field*."

"Wow! I get it." Then Kenny frowned. "I still don't know how my friends are going to understand this."

"Don't worry about what your friends understand. All that matters is what *you* understand. If you focus on them feeling separate from everything else, then you will perceive them as separate. If you focus on seeing them through the Lens of Love, you will feel connected to them and perceive them to be connected to the whole. Remember, your perception is your reality. That means your perception of them is your reality too."

# Chapter 8
## New Teachers Emerge

As the weeks passed by, Kenny and James shared more stories with the other patients. Each of them seemed to process the information in different ways. The questions that the other patients asked got more and more complex. When Kenny or James couldn't answer a question, they went back to Leo and Carlos for guidance. Kenny was very pleased with how things were progressing. He was personally feeling stronger each day, and everyone in the group appeared to have more energy despite the rigorous treatments they were going through. Much to Kenny's delight, his bond with James continued to strengthen.

"It's amazing how James and I are always in sync," he said to Carlos one evening.

"What do you mean by that?" Carlos replied.

"You know, we have a connection. We're always on the same wavelength. We think the same."

"You mean you have similar thoughts?"

"Exactly! That's what it feels like," Kenny exclaimed.

"That's very interesting."

"What?"

"That you recognized that you and James were in sync, but you never used that term to describe us. Yet that is exactly what we are. We are in sync, you and I."

"In what way?" asked Kenny.

"In exactly the way you described being in sync with James. There is a connection between us. We are on the same wavelength, or the same vibrational frequency. We are able to intimately share our thoughts. That is what being in sync is all about."

Kenny considered this. "I never thought of it that way. Are others in sync too?"

"Being in sync is being in harmony or unity with something or someone else. Every creature in your universe inherently seeks this unity…this harmony…of being in sync. It's nice to know that you are in sync with James."

"It's nice to know that I am in sync with you."

"Yes, that too."

❧  ❧  ❧

One of the things James missed the most from home was planting in his garden. He had developed it over time to include many different types of garden variety vegetables. That used to be his little oasis where he could forget about the outside world. He loved planting the seeds, nurturing the garden, and reaping the fruits of his labor.

At *H.E.A.R.T.* he would stare out the window of the Community Room at the patch of grass that separated the walking path from the large outside fence. He drew a picture in his mind of which vegetables he would plant there and he would imagine taking care of them every day. He also shared his love of planting with Leo, which resulted in many delightful conversations.

One afternoon, he was looking out the window when Stevie came over and asked him what he was looking at.

"My garden," said James nonchalantly.

"What garden?" asked Stevie.

"The one growing right over there."

"Is it an imaginary garden?" Stevie asked with skepticism. "Because I can't see it."

"It's still a garden, isn't it?"

Stevie thought about this. "Why don't you make a real one?"

"I couldn't do that," said James defensively.

"Why not?"

"They would never let me."

"Have you ever asked?"

James paused. "No," he finally answered.

"So, what are you waiting for?"

James got very excited. He thought about how he would justify creating a garden right outside of the Community Room. He spoke to his parents and explained what he wanted to do. His parents went to the staff at *H.E.A.R.T.* and made the request for him.

A week later, his parents relayed the decision. He was not allowed to create a vegetable garden on the H.E.A.R.T. property. James' heart sank.

"But," said his father, "they will let you plant flowers outside the Community Room."

James was ecstatic. He did not have the strength to build much of a flowerbed, but he planted what he could and began the wait for the results to sprout from the ground. That night, he shared the good news with Leo. He explained how he loved to plant seeds and watch them grow. Leo then explained how it was similar to the concept of the mirror. The flower seeds that James planted in the ground must produce those same flowers. Similarly, he reasoned, the image that James projected into the mirror had to be the same image reflected back to him.

The next day, James shared this new found wisdom with his friends. As usual, Kenny took in all the information and then went back to Carlos with more questions.

"James shared something very interesting with us today."

"What was that?" asked Carlos.

"James said he was telling Leo about the seeds that he was allowed to plant and then Leo reminded him it is not very different than the concept of the mirror. He said the seeds that he planted are like the mirror. It must produce what's planted … just like the mirror must reflect what it's shown. Is that true? Are we like seeds?

"Yes and no."

Kenny closed his eyes and shook his head back and forth. "There you go again. Can't you ever just give me a simple answer?"

"There is a simple yes and a simple no."

"Okay. What is the simple 'yes'?"

"Yes, the seed is very much like the mirror. It must produce what it is designed to produce. It never deviates from that. It is a perfect code, if you want to think of it like a computer program."

"That makes sense," said Kenny, "and I understand the correlation between the reflection in the mirror and the germination of the seeds. So why did you say there's also a 'no'?"

"The seed has a perfect code. We'll call it 'nature's code' and it can never change. Your human code works the same … except for one factor."

"What's that?" Kenny asked.

"Humans can change the code. A plant cannot. A tomato seed must always become a tomato. But humans can change their projection of who they are being … and that changes the reflection in the mirror."

"How do we change our code?"

"By changing how you feel. For example, every time you feel love, you rewrite the program and start attracting what you want into your life. But if you focus on not having what you want, you see through the Lens of Fear, and your life reflects the absence of what you want."

"So, I'm not like the seed because I can change who I am … and the seed can't?"

"That is correct," confirmed Carlos.

"But James was right because the seed is like the mirror, since the seed must become what is planted in the ground and the mirror must reflect what is shown to it."

"You are correct again."

Kenny felt good that he and James could bounce ideas off Carlos and Leo. They continued to encourage the other patients to look within for their own answers. After a while, it seemed like it was starting to work.

The Community Room was a place where the friends could share ideas with each other. It was also a place where they could enjoy time for themselves when they weren't going through arduous treatments. For Stevie, she could always be found in the Community Room wearing one of her trademark bandanas. She stored her collection of bandanas in her room where she kept them on the top shelf. She never explained why she loved them so much but her friends assumed it was because it camouflaged the lack of hair on her head. She also found joy in anything associated with computers. She loved computer games and she also enjoyed creating programs and watching them follow her commands. Her favorite was creating fractal patterns. She loved to see them continuously replicate themselves. It was something that she could control in her life.

One afternoon, Kenny asked her why she liked fractal patterns so much. He was surprised by Stevie's answer.

"It's like when you talk about the *Lens of Love* or the *Lens of Fear*," Stevie replied.

"What do you mean?" responded Kenny, somewhat startled.

"Your feeling is the code," Stevie explained. "The code to the fractal pattern that you initiate. Feel anger and that pattern will keep repeating in every aspect of your life. Same with guilt. Feel love and appreciation and that pattern will keep repeating in every aspect of your life as well."

Other patients overheard Stevie and they started to slide their chairs closer so they could better hear her. As they started to gather around, Stevie continued:

"This whole simulation that we call life is a fractal pattern based on a simple recursive code. It's like a hologram that keeps recreating the same image of itself. The only way to change that image, and what keeps repeating, is by changing the feeling that created that image in the first place."

"Go on," said James with a deepening sense of curiosity.

"Change the feeling and you create a new pattern. You keep experiencing that pattern, or simulation, as long as you maintain that feeling. Our experience of life is based on the simulation we're running. Too often we let the simulation determine how we feel and that emotion becomes the input into the pattern that drives the simulation. But if we understand that we can choose a different emotion to use as the input for the code, then a new pattern emerges, one that we desire … and that pattern continues to reproduce itself in the same image."

"You're saying we all run our own simulation code?" Kenny interjected.

"Yes," confirmed Stevie.

"… and that simulation code is determined by the emotion or feeling that we use in the beginning of that code?" Kenny continued.

"Yes again."

"And if I feel the joy and gratitude of being completely healed, that goes into the code I've created and it runs the program that I am healed?" Kenny concluded.

"Bingo."

"It sounds like wishful thinking," said Danny.

"It's not 'wishing'," Stevie replied. "It's just a program or a pattern repeating itself. Where we all get tripped up is that we change the input when we change our emotions, so the program has to change as well. Of course, we don't realize that we were the ones who changed the program, so we just stop believing that we have control over our own program."

Stevie continued without pausing. "But once we recognize the correlation of our emotions to the specific program or pattern it creates, then we finally start to understand how the whole process works. We start to understand that the process doesn't just control the cells in our body … it controls all the cells in the universe, because they're all connected."

There was a long pause.

Stevie looked at all her friends staring at her in stunned silence. "What" she asked.

"Where did you come up with that?" asked Kenny incredulously.

"I derived it from what Leo and Carlos were telling you guys."

"I never even thought you were paying attention to us," said James.

"Of course, I was. I was just processing all that information."

⚜ ⚜ ⚜

That night, Kenny shared with Carlos what Stevie had explained during the day. "She said our feelings create the program of our life."

"That is true," said Carlos.

"I understand what she's saying, but can I really create my own programs so they always produce the results I want?"

"Let me ask you a question. When Stevie writes a computer program, do you think she expects it to run the exact way that she set it up?"

"If she set it up correctly, sure. She would know exactly how it was going to run."

"Is it the same for you in real life?" asked Carlos.

"What do you mean?"

"When you set an intention for something to happen, do you always expect it to happen?"

Kenny thought about this. "Not always … but sometimes."

"Why not always?"

Kenny shrugged. "I don't know. A lot of things are just out of my control."

Carlos knew that wasn't true. "Nothing is ever out of your control. You just believe it is. But if you were able to write the specific program to produce something you wanted in your life, you would always be able to expect it. It's because the pattern or program doesn't change on its own. It just reflects exactly what it was shown.

Just like the mirror and just like the garden. Remember, the mirror doesn't reflect something different back to you, and the garden doesn't grow something different from the seeds that were planted. You expect to see what you show to the mirror. You expect the seed to grow what you planted. You expect the computer program to run as it was designed. True?"

Kenny paused. "Yes, true."

"For your life, you write the program with your intentions. You run the program with your emotions. Those are the inputs and you must expect the program to run based on the inputs."

"But what if I don't make any inputs," said Kenny. "Does the program still run?"

"It sure does. The program is always running. It's just using the inputs that you have picked up from other people throughout your life."

"What inputs are those?"

"You don't remember when you were just a child," said Carlos, "but I do. I couldn't get through to you because you just kept downloading information from everything you heard and saw. After a while, I wasn't sure we would ever be able to communicate like we do now. Do you remember any of the things that you might have picked up from what other people used to say about you?"

Kenny started to recall some of the things he repeatedly heard from others. "Yeah...they said things like 'look at the little weakling over there'...and 'are you sure he's not sick?'"

"Did you believe them?" asked Carlos.

"Not at first. But after a while...sure...some of them started to affect what I believed."

"Do you think those programs had any effect on how things turned out?"

"I guess it's possible," Kenny admitted.

"Then it is possible for new programs to have an effect on how things turn out in the future. The good news is now you have a choice. You can keep running the same programs that you picked up from others in the past, or we can create new ones to produce new outcomes that are more appealing to you in the future."

"Yes. I'm all for that. Wait – let me guess. Feelings are the language of the program."

"Why would it be anything else?" Carlos responded. "Your feeling states are the results of your thoughts plus your emotions. It's the same as your beliefs. So, if you want to change the program, change your beliefs. If you want to change your beliefs, change how you think and feel."

⚜ ⚜ ⚜

Kenny stretched out in his chair while he sat in the Community Room waiting to play video games with his friends. It was rare that they all felt up to playing on the same day. Someone was always in treatment or feeling the negative effects of them. Stevie was the one person they didn't play without. They already had a newfound appreciation for her after her interpretation of fractal patterns. Now she was helping each one of them to create their own avatars so they could all play the same video game at the same time. Kenny rarely won these games but he enjoyed them immensely. It was a time in the day when he was able to lose himself in the game and become the avatar. They all needed to be able to take a break from the harshness of their daily routine of treatments and medication. Video games were a big help.

After playing multiple video games throughout the afternoon, Kenny returned to his room and immediately started contemplating his relationship with the avatar that he created and how he used the avatar to move around in the game. He controlled the avatar like he controlled his own body. The more he thought about it, the more he realized he needed to reach out to Carlos for some validation on this symbiotic relationship with his avatar. He went over to his black chair where he could best summon him up.

"I've been thinking a lot about my body," he shared with Carlos. "If I'm only temporarily in this body, who am I really?"

"You are an eternal being who has manifested in your physical body in order to experience your Self. You just think that you are a separate human being trying to figure out life by yourself with no connection to the very consciousness from which you came. Everything you experience is based on your perception of it ... either seeing from the perspective of your eternal being – that's me – or from other people's perspective that you have adopted as your own. How was that? Too much for you?" Carlos concluded.

"Not at all. What you're saying is that I'm really like an avatar in a video game."

"And how are you like an avatar?" Carlos asked.

"When I play video games with the guys, the avatar I've created takes guidance from me, who appears separate from the game but is really very much a part of it. And I'm always steering the avatar in the right direction because I can see things that the avatar can't see. I'm like the avatar's conscience, and at the same time, we're one and the same. The avatar is made in the image of me, and when the game's over, I still exist regardless of what happened to the avatar in the game. Likewise, I'm in this human body taking guidance from you, who appears separate from me but is really very much a part of this game of life. We're still one in the same, and you are always trying to steer me towards the best possible outcomes. Regardless of what happens to me in this lifetime, you will still exist when the game is over."

Carlos was duly impressed. "That is quite the analogy," he said.

"Is it accurate?" Kenny asked.

"You could not have made it more accurate. We came from the *Field* and now we are temporarily in this *Land,* and you can actually observe yourself in this *Land* before we go back to the *Field.* You're right: it's like you observing yourself in a computer game. In the video game, you create a digital version of yourself, which is the avatar, and place it in a realistic yet simulated environment. Then you observe yourself moving around the simulation game. You can even influence what the avatar does. But no matter what happens to the avatar in the game, you are still unchanged as the observer. In this game of life that we are playing, it's the same concept. I am the non-physical part of us that you can tune into, and we can observe this human experience we are having. And no matter what happens to your physical body, in the end you are still unchanged as the observer, because you are I and I am you.

"I thought so," said Kenny with a big smile. "Thanks."

The Community Room was not just used for playing video games. Danny spent the majority of his time tuning into various frequencies with his old-fashioned two-way radio. There was a radio tower a few miles away that only marginally aided his radio's reception. No one actively utilized it anymore…with the possible exception of Danny.

One afternoon, Danny adjusted his thick black glasses as he tinkered with the different frequencies. He smiled with excitement as a faint voice broke through the static. It was someone speaking in a foreign language. Danny pretended that he could understand the person he was making contact with. He started a dialogue with the voice as if it were responding directly to him.

"What's he saying?" asked Kenny.

"He's saying that he has been searching for me his whole life," replied Danny.

"Yeah, right," said James.

Danny ignored James' pessimism and kept pretending to converse with his new found acquaintance.

"Forget what he's saying," Stevie interjected. "How's that voice getting here?"

"It's just tuning into our frequency," replied Danny.

"How many different frequencies are there?"

"I don't know if we'll ever know. Let's just say a lot. Their signal can come through the radio tower, but my body is also like an antenna. Danny instinctively straightened his body up. I can pick up all different types of frequencies."

Kenny's head snapped up and he stared at Danny. "What did you say?"

"I'm an antenna. Each cell in my body is like a transmitter, constantly sending and receiving signals."

Kenny was stunned. "That's what Carlos told me."

"Cool," said Danny with a new air of confidence.

Kenny didn't know how to respond so he didn't say anything more. Before going to bed that night, he addressed it directly with Carlos.

"How did he know that?" Kenny said curtly. "He said that he was like an antenna...and that each cell in his body was like a transmitter. That's what you told me, and I never told anyone else. Are people spying on our conversations?"

Carlos realized this was new territory for him to teach Kenny, so he tried to be as clear as he could. "Everything we think and communicate to each other is just a vibration stored in the *Field* as energy. Everyone has access to it. Danny accessed the *Field* and retrieved it."

"You mean everything we talk about is open to everyone?"

"Yes. Everything."

"That's crazy!" Kenny squeezed the top of his head with both hands as he tried to make sense of what he was hearing.

Carlos knew this was difficult for him to grasp, so he decided to change his approach. "Where am I, Kenny?"

"What?"

"Where am I?"

"In the *Field*?"

"Yes," said Carlos. "And when we are in communion, where is the frequency you are tapping into?"

"In the *Field*."

"That's right. Now, are you the only human who can access the *Field*?"

"No. Anyone can access the *Field* if they raise their vibrations high enough."

"That's right. So why would you think that any other human would not be able to access thoughts you have placed in the *Field*?"

"Whoa!" Kenny exclaimed. "Hold on! Are you saying that *any* human has access to conversations we have?"

"Yes."

"But they can't hear us!"

"What are our internal conversations? They're just thoughts. Those thoughts are stored in the *Field* just like everyone else's thoughts. That *Field* is consciousness, and since everyone has access to it, that has become part of the collective consciousness."

Kenny found himself in a vast ocean of swirling thoughts. He closed his eyes and eventually he drifted off to sleep without another word.

# CHAPTER 9
## JUST BE ME

The next morning, Kenny couldn't stop thinking about the collective consciousness. He lay in bed and murmured, "I still can't believe everyone has access to our conversations."

"Look at the bright side," Carlos responded. "You have access to everyone else's conversations too."

"How do I even know that what you're saying is true?"

"It only matters if it's true for you. But if you really need to know, everything we've talked about will eventually be proven by your scientists. In the meantime, they will have a lot of fun trying to prove how so many of you are doing things you're not supposed to be able to do."

"Things like people healing themselves?" asked Kenny.

"Yes."

"You really think they'll be able to prove it some day?"

"They already have," said Carlos. "They just have to remember what they already knew."

"What do you mean?"

"Do you think you're the first civilization on this planet to understand the laws of the universe?"

"No," said Kenny. "But I thought we've gotten the furthest along."

"Sorry to disappoint you."

"How is that possible?"

"Man has essentially had to start over many times," said Carlos.

"So you're saying there have been humans before us who could heal cancer?"

"Not only could they heal cancer, but they didn't need machines to do it."

"Then why is this taking us so long?" Kenny asked.

"There you go worrying about time again."

"I'm not worrying about it. I just want to be healthy. I'm doing what you say. So why isn't it happening?"

"Kenny, focusing on who you want to be is so important, because it is far more powerful than focusing on who you are not. But who you *want* to be is not enough. It's just a stepping-stone to who you *are* being. If you always stay in the 'I want to be' mindset, you will always be one step behind becoming who you want to be. Once you decide who you want to be, you must *become* that person, because the *Field* doesn't reflect back to you who you *want* to be. The *Field* only reflects back to you who you are *being*."

"I don't know who I am being right now," said Kenny. "You keep telling me that I have the power within me to become healthy. But it's not happening. Is this all a lie? Can you make me healthy or not? If you can really make me healthy, then just do it! I'm sick and tired of being sick and tired!"

"Kenny. You are already healthy but you can't see it. You see one 'you' going through life and that 'you' is sick and tired. I see a field of potential *you's*. You all exist simultaneously, waiting for you to experience yourself."

"If there are many potential *me's*, which one do I experience?"

"The one you choose to be."

"How do I choose?" asked Kenny.

"It's the one you are being in any moment. That is who you have chosen to be, whether you are aware of it or not."

"I want to experience the healthy me," Kenny declared.

"Do you really want to know why you do not experience what you want to experience?"

"Yes," Kenny said immediately.

"Okay. This is what keeps happening: first, you desire something or imagine something that you would like, such as being healthy. You reinforce it by repeating, 'I am healthy.'"

"Yes, because that's what you told me to do!"

"That's right," said Carlos. "And I always become what you desire to be. No exceptions. So now I'm healthy too. But then, before it has a chance to show up in your physical reality, you start to doubt it. You focus on the absence of what you desire, because you haven't seen it yet. As the doubt kicks in and you keep saying, 'I am not,' I must now become the absence of what you desire, because that is who you are being in this moment. In other words, by repeatedly thinking and believing, 'I am not healthy,' you are forcing me to no longer be healthy. Since we are no longer in sync, I change who I am in order to keep reflecting who you are being. The irony, Kenny, is that if you knew beyond a shadow of a doubt that we already became what you desire to be, you would never start to doubt it, because doubting it must take it away."

"What do you mean 'doubting it must take it away'?"

"By doubting it, you are no longer being it, and if you are no longer being it, then I can no longer be it either because the *Field* is just reflecting back who you are being. So, it is never me who stops being who you desire to be. It is always you who makes the first move. I only stop being healthy when you stop believing you are healthy."

"*You* may be healthy but I'm not!" Kenny exclaimed. "Why can't you just heal me! You have all the power, don't you?"

"Kenny, all the power in the world has always been with you."

"How can you say that?"

"You have been blessed with the power of free will."

Kenny paused. "What do you mean the power of free will?"

"Free will means you have a choice, and everything in your experience of life comes down to one choice."

"What's that?"

"To be me or not to be me."

Kenny nodded. "I remember. You're saying that in every moment, I am you or I am not you."

"That's exactly what I'm saying. When you repeat the words 'I am you,' you are strengthening your awareness of being me. 'I am not' is the absence of it. So, you are either aware of being me or you are not aware of being me. It's your choice. It's your free will."

"It's not so easy to just be you. It's like being my own conscience."

"Everything is consciousness, Kenny. Your whole world was created by consciousness because your whole world is consciousness. I am the consciousness of love. So, if you have one choice, to be me or not to be me, why would you ever choose not to be me? Why would you ever choose the absence of being conscious of love?"

"I might not choose the absence of being you, but what if I just stopped being you?"

"You can't stop being me, Kenny. You can only stop being aware of being me. I'm not going anywhere. I am always right here and I am you. You must believe that."

"I do believe that," said Kenny. "I believe that I'm you because I know I'm communicating with you right now. I just have trouble believing that you've already become everything I want."

"Do you believe that everything you desire is a potential probability?"

"Yeah, but even if it's a potential probability, that doesn't mean it is going to happen."

"Okay. But if you have any desire, it's a potential probability … right?"

"Yeah, but …." Kenny couldn't finish his thought.

"No 'buts.' It's just one simple question. Is it a potential probability?"

"Yes," Kenny acknowledged.

"And all potential probabilities must exist somewhere?"

"I suppose they exist in the *Field of Potential Probabilities*?"

"That is correct. Every one of those potential probabilities, or your desires, already exists in the *Field*. I have already become every one of them, and since I am you, you have already become what you desire to be. So just be me and that is what must be reflected back to you from the field."

A feeling of calm overtook Kenny's body…and then the revelation came. He sat right up and said out loud, "I know who I want to be!"

"Who do you want to be?" responded Carlos.

"I want to be you."

❧ ❧ ❧

Throughout the day, Kenny kept imagining himself as an eternal being. He could see his life before him and it was a life beyond the four walls of *H.E.A.R.T.* He kept trying to imagine where he would go if he left *H.E.A.R.T.* When he went to the cafeteria for lunch, he saw his friends talking, so he sat down beside them. As he listened to their conversation for a while, he kept picturing all of them laughing together outside of the four walls that currently occupied all of their time. If it wasn't realistic, it didn't matter. It certainly felt real in that moment. Finally, he turned to them and asked, "Any of you guys ever think about walking out of this hospital for good?"

"No," said Danny.

"I wish," added Stevie.

Kenny leaned in further and spoke in a low tone. "That's what I mean. Do you ever wish you could just walk out the front door all healthy?"

This time Danny laughed out loud. "Sure, but that doesn't mean it's going to happen."

Kenny continued with the same train of thought. "Let me do something crazy. Let's all pretend that we will walk out of this hospital completely healed…even if it's not at the same time."

"I can do that," said Stevie.

"And then when we do," Kenny continued, "suppose we all want to meet up somewhere. Where do we want to meet?"

"I know," said James. "Let's go to my neck of the woods and meet at the Cliffs of Molly. It has the most breathtaking views you'll ever see, overlooking the ocean."

"Works for me," said Stevie. "I don't know how we're going to be able to top that."

Everyone agreed.

"Well then, the Cliffs of Molly it is," declared James. "When we all walk out of this place, I'll meet you at the Cliffs."

Kenny couldn't contain his smile. "I'll see you all there."

The four friends put their hands together and then raised them over their heads. "To the Cliffs of Molly!" they all shouted.

Kenny was pleased with the response of his three friends. He knew that they would need to keep that vision alive in their minds and hearts if they were going to make it a reality. He was sure that he was up to the challenge. He was not as confident about his friends.

⚜   ⚜   ⚜

Kenny poured himself a cup of water and made his way over to his favorite chair in his room. He looked through the window to an overcast sky that bore a striking resemblance to his current mood. He kept thinking about the conversation with his friends and how they all got to this point in their lives. How many of them would make it to the Cliffs of Molly? He thought about all the negative things people had said to him and how those words made him feel. It wasn't a comfortable feeling.

He shifted his attention to Carlos and decided to ask for some help. "I know I've never had a strong self-image, but I'd like to change that."

"Then change it," Carlos replied.

"You always make things sound so easy, but it's hard."

"Your self-image is your self-imagination. Self-imagination is just imagining yourself to be who you desire yourself to be. That's fun to do, Kenny. So if you want to change your life, then change that image … because the reflection can't change until the projection changes … and your self-image is the projection of who you are being."

"But how can imagining myself to be healthy actually change my body to be healthy?" Kenny wondered out loud.

"Your self-imagination creates a new 'future memory' about yourself, and your 'future memory' then stores new information in your cells … which passes that new information onto future cells … which in turn creates a whole new 'you'."

"What's a future memory?" Kenny asked.

"If a past memory is just an image of a past experience in your mind, then a future memory is just an image of a future experience in your mind."

"Where does that future image come from?" asked Kenny.

"It is your imagination."

"You're telling me that my imagination is a future memory?"

"That is exactly what I am telling you."

"If it's a future memory, that means it's already happened."

"Yes, it has," Carlos confirmed. "It has already happened in the *Field*. But don't worry, if you hold onto that future memory long enough … your physical experience will catch up to it."

"How can it have already happened if it's in the future?"

"Back up for a minute," said Carlos. "Let *me* ask *you* a question. Is there something you have thought about in your imagination so many times that you can feel as if it has already happened?

Kenny considered this. "Yes."

"Can you remember thinking about it yesterday?"

Kenny thought about that image and how many times he replayed it in his mind. There wasn't a day that went by when he didn't think about it.

"Yes, I remember that image."

"You are remembering your future. What is that image that you are remembering?"

"I'm walking out of the front door of *H.E.A.R.T*....wearing a red shirt...waving goodbye to my friends...and I'm completely healthy."

"Does that memory feel real?" asked Carlos.

"Absolutely."

"Close your eyes and tell me if you can picture it and feel it right now."

Kenny closed his eyes. "Yes, I can," he stated calmly.

As he said those words, a huge smile broke out across his face. In that moment, he realized that the vision in his mind felt so real because it was a future memory. It had already happened in the *Field*. He knew that if he kept focusing on that image through the Lens of Love, it would be reflected back to him from the *Field*. That image was as clear to him as any memory he'd ever had.

"This is amazing," he said. "How can I see it so clearly now?"

"You're using your third eye," responded Carlos.

"Very funny. You're saying I have three eyes in my head?"

"Not three physical eyes. But accessing your third eye allows you to see images that you don't see with your other eyes. It allows you to access images in the *Field*."

Kenny furrowed his brow. "Do I only see good images with the third eye?"

"You can see any kind of image you want. For example, can you picture a scenario where you are not healed? Where you stay sick in this hospital?

"Sure. That's not too difficult."

"Now you have two different pictures, or two different images in your mind. One image is where you are healed and walking out the front door. The other image is where you are still sick. Would you agree that they are two different potential probabilities?"

"Yes! They're potential probabilities. Now I get it! They're both waiting for me in the *Field*!"

"You got it!" said Carlos. "You just need to decide which image you would like to experience."

"Of course, I'd like to experience the scenario where I'm completely healed," Kenny declared.

"Then hold onto that image. How does it make you feel?"

"I feel excited. I feel grateful."

"Excellent. Now hold onto those feelings. Let that become the dominant image you see and feel all through the day… every day."

"I can do that," Kenny replied confidently.

"You will find it is more challenging than you think to hold onto that feeling because you will keep being pulled away by other images you see and feel in the *Land.* But if you are persistent in returning to this image as if it has already happened, that future memory becomes the program that you run every day in your subconscious mind."

"Wow! I get it! Thank you."

⚜ ⚜ ⚜

Over the next few weeks, that was the image Kenny kept returning to: the image of him walking out of the hospital with a red shirt on. That future memory seemed to energize him. He felt stronger every day and it seemed to be rubbing off on his friends too. Kenny couldn't imagine things going any better.

His parents noticed a change in his demeanor as well. As they sat in his room one afternoon while he was getting x-rays taken, there was a calm feeling that they rarely experienced in the hospital. It was a feeling of hope… even though they couldn't quite identify its origin.

"I'm glad he seems so positive lately," his mother commented to his dad. "Are you seeing the same thing as me?"

"Yes, I am," his father responded. "I don't know where the change is coming from but I hope it continues."

"We're supposed to be the strong ones," his mother replied. "Somehow, I feel like I am getting strength from him."

"Me too," said his father. "It's crazy, but I am starting to expect him to get better."

His wife smiled at him. The thought of Kenny getting better was overwhelming to her. She wished she could maintain that feeling of hopefulness on a consistent basis. Too often, her feelings resembled more of a roller-coaster than a steady calm. For now, she would wallow in the feeling of the steady calm.

Kenny started to settle into a regular routine. Each night he would fall asleep thinking about Carlos. He was very grateful for their communication. When he awoke in the morning, he focused on the two things Carlos asked him to do: be consciously aware of his breath, and to feel only love. This immediately put him in a state of communion with Carlos. The more he asked questions, the stronger their connection grew.

"Thank you for this understanding mind and understanding heart," he said to Carlos one morning.

"That is what you asked for," Carlos replied. "You believed in its coming...and you received it. So, what did you learn?"

"Well, I asked for an understanding mind and I'm finally starting to really understand."

"What do you understand?" asked Carlos.

"I understand that I am the manifest version of you. It's not enough for me to know that you are a vibrational being and that you reside in the *Field*. I know that I am you. I finally get it that I'm here so you can experience yourself, and you are full of love and joy, so you can only experience it through me if that's what I'm feeling. Even if I don't feel like being happy for myself – usually because of some conditions I'm using as the reason for not being able to feel good – I will be happy for you. That's my gift to you, Carlos. That's my gift to my Self! I will give you the feeling of joy."

Carlos was pleased. "I couldn't ask for more than that."

"I just wish I could maintain that happiness all the time," Kenny admitted.

"Why can't you?"

"I always get a little scared thinking about the future."

"Do not fear the unknown. Where do you want to be in ten years?" Carlos asked.

Kenny couldn't picture anything that far out. "I just want to be alive."

"If you knew you were going to be alive, where would you want to be?"

"It wouldn't matter. I just want to be happy. The doctors say there's no way I'm going to live that long … but I'm okay with that now."

"Your future-self does not agree with that."

"Now I have a future-self?"

"Yes," said Carlos. "That's you in five years, ten years, or any timeframe from right now that you want to make it."

"Now you can talk to my future-self too?"

"Of course. If I am you, then I am also your future-self."

"Then what's my future-self saying right now?

"He's saying to you, 'If you can imagine it, then I already did it.'"

"I'm having a little trouble believing my future-self is here."

Carlos shifted his approach again. "Let's start over. Do you believe that I am here with you right now?"

"Well, yeah, I'm communicating with you right now."

"Which means we are in communion."

"Whatever."

"I am here with you right now, correct?" Carlos asked again.

"Yes," said Kenny with little enthusiasm.

"How about yesterday? Was I with you yesterday when you were given ice cream for dessert?"

"Yes. You had to have been there because you know we had ice cream."

"That's right," said Carlos. "I was there and the ice cream was good. Let me ask you this: Will I be with you tomorrow when you will be spending time with your parents?"

"I guess so."

"Do you guess so or do you really believe that I will be here with you tomorrow?"

"Okay. I really believe you will be with me tomorrow."

"So, your 'past-self' ate ice cream and I was there with you. There is your 'present-self' and I am right here with you now. There is your 'future-self' and I will be with you here tomorrow. Correct?"

"I never thought about there being three of me. But yes, I guess you could say I have a past-self, a present-self and a future-self," Kenny admitted.

Carlos continued. "What separates those three people?"

"I don't know. Time?"

"Yes, but it is your *perception* of time. So, the difference between those three *you's* is your perception of time. What is the same between all three of you? What do you all have in common?"

Kenny thought about this. "I'm not sure."

"What do all three of you share?"

"You?"

"Exactly! The only thing separating all three of you is your perception of time, and one thing uniting all three of you is your connection to me."

"Wow!"

"So now here comes the big question. What is the difference between you and me?"

"I'm real and you're not?" Kenny asked sarcastically.

"Of course, I'm real. Otherwise, we wouldn't be having this conversation."

"Okay, what's the difference between us? Besides the fact that I'm a physical being and you're an eternal being."

"The difference between us is that you separate your three selves into three different people: your past-self, your present-self and your future-self. But I am all three of those people right now. I am all three of you right now. Your experience of being those three people is separated by your perception of time and space. It is three different points of consciousness for you. My experience of being those three people is happening simultaneously, and since I am you, you can experience all three *you's* simultaneously too."

"And how am I supposed to do that?" Kenny asked.

"I am your future-self who stays sick and I am your future-self who gets well. I am all of your potential future selves. You choose which one you want to experience based on how you feel and what you believe right now. If you believe it, and you feel it, I express it."

Kenny raised an eyebrow. "You want me to just tell myself that I'm healed?"

"Saying it is a good start – but remember: if you say it and doubt it, then you have negated it. Instead, if you say it over and over and you start to believe it, then you start to feel as if you are healed. You are then raising your vibration to equal that of your future-self who is already healed. Remember, I have already become all of your future selves. I'm just waiting to express the one you are being right now."

"I remember this, but you may have to keep going over it again."

"Kenny, do you understand how I can be all three of your selves at the same time?"

"I'm trying. I really am."

"Okay, let's go slower," said Carlos. "I came from the Field and we are sharing this experience in this *Land of Perception and Time*. You can change your past experience, present experience and future experience on Gaia by simply changing your perception of it. Since your perception of it is the lens through which you observe it, then your perception can match my perception by seeing through the same lens through which I am observing this *Land*."

"Yes, I know," said Kenny. "The Lens of Love. So that's what you came here to do – but what about what *I* want to do? What about what I want for my future-self?"

"Your imagination is what you want for your future-self."

Kenny closed his eyes and took a deep breath. "Let me try to get this straight. Since you're connected to my future-self and my imagination is my future-self…then my imagination is the path between my present-self and my future-self."

"Keep going," Carlos encouraged.

"This means I need to focus on the alignment of my present-self and you…and if I can imagine who I want my future-self to be, then I can be that person."

Carlos waited for him to continue.

"My future-self is already connected to you," said Kenny, "just as my present-self is connected to you and my past-self is connected to you. I can change my past by perceiving it through your eyes. I can change my present by perceiving it through your eyes. And I can change my future by perceiving it through your eyes as well."

"Yes!" Carlos exclaimed. He was excited that Kenny was really starting to understand his perception of reality.

Carlos continued, "I am all of your selves simultaneously, so by aligning with me now and imagining what you would like your future-self to be, I have already become it – because I am your future-self too. And whatever you perceive your future-self to be is what your future-self will be."

Kenny sighed. "I want my future-self to be healthy, but it's taking so long."

"Kenny, listen closely because this is really important. There is a gap between you imagining yourself to be healthy and your body physically becoming healthy. But there is not a gap between you imagining yourself to be healthy and me becoming healthy. If you can imagine it, then I have become it. Just trust me. The more you enjoy the gap, the faster you will become what I already am. It is law."

⚜   ⚜   ⚜

It was late in the afternoon and the full staff of *H.E.A.R.T.* gathered for their bi-monthly staff meeting. The half-filled auditorium was a multi-purpose room with fifteen rows of seats cascading down to a small stage in the center of the room. *H.E.A.R.T.*'s Chief of Staff, Dr. Lee, was preparing to start the meeting as the final few staff members found their seats. Dr. Lee was a tall, lean man with streaks of gray in his otherwise black hair. As he surveyed the room, he adjusted his blue silk tie before delivering his opening remarks.

When he was finished with his overview, each of the doctors discussed the latest treatments that they were giving the patients, along with some of the success rates of those treatments. The improvements shown were not across the board, but the doctors were very encouraged with the results they were seeing. As they went through each of the patients and shared their progress, a young blond-haired intern named Emily started to jot down notes on a pad of paper. She had been observing Kenny and his friends in the Community Room and she found the latest test results very intriguing. When the updates were finished, she stepped forward somewhat hesitantly to ask a question.

"Excuse me, but I just have to ask something, even though this may seem a bit far-fetched."

"Please go on," said Dr. Lee.

"As you went through the list of patients who were showing improvements, and those who weren't showing improvements, I noticed they seem to fall into two different categories."

"And what categories are those?" asked the Chief of Staff.

"The list of patients showing the most improvement are predominantly those patients from the section I've been working in."

"That's very nice to hear, Miss Gladwell, but are you suggesting you've had something specific to do with the positive results in your section?"

She shook her head. "That's the point. No, I'm not."

"I'm not sure I follow you," replied Dr. Lee.

"Umm…you see…I've noticed something very unusual over the last few months. One of our patients, named Kenny Haneg, has been sharing stories with a lot of the other patients in our section. It started out with a couple of patients just meeting in his room every few days, but now it's grown into regular gatherings in the Community Room."

"And what do they do at these regular gatherings?"

She shrugged. "Not much. Mostly they just talk. But it's what they talk about."

"And that is…?"

"They talk about all of them coming from a field, and that they were all connected when they were in this field."

"What's so special about this field?" asked one of the doctors from the third row.

"It is a field of energy... and they believe they can all get better when they connect to this field."

The noise level in the room rose instantly as Emily shared her observations.

"Let's keep it down," Dr. Lee shouted as he tried to grasp what the intern was telling him. "And why didn't you come to us sooner with this information, Miss Gladwell?"

"I didn't think there was any harm to it," she said. "They were upbeat when they were talking about it. It seemed to make them feel happy, and when you're constantly caring for patients who are struggling through life-threatening illnesses as well as the side effects of these powerful drugs we're giving them, it was comforting to see a smile on their face. Just to be clear, I'm not saying this is the sole reason why this group of patients has outperformed all the other groups. But I do think it's a very interesting coincidence."

After a somewhat lengthy discussion about the many possible scenarios for one section showing more positive results than others, Dr. Lee spoke up:

"It's obvious we aren't going to come to any finite conclusions here right now, so let's just say it is encouraging for our hospital to show increased results, and let's keep monitoring these developments closely."

The meeting was adjourned.

# CHAPTER 10
# DOUBTING THOMAS

Thomas lay in his bed at *H.E.A.R.T.* His mind drifted back to another time where he'd also been lying in bed. He could remember hearing his parents arguing. His father had raised his voice at his mom: "If it weren't for your side of the family we wouldn't be here. You know as well as I do, he inherited these genes from you. Everyone in your family has some kind of sickness. My whole family is healthy. All our plans for the future are now tied up with helping the sick side of the family."

"That is heartless!" his mother had shot back. "And not even true!"

The arguing had continued. It was the same pattern that repeated itself over and over. His mother knew her husband's anger wasn't because of Thomas and his illness. It had started long before he was born. She remembered when he blamed her parents for 'ruining' their prom night because they wouldn't let her stay out all night. Then he blamed her parents for 'ruining' their honeymoon because they wouldn't pay for the airfare to a tropical island. His 'blame game' never really stopped. Thomas had just replaced her parents as the recipient of his anger and became someone new to blame.

During the argument, her frustration with her husband built to a boiling point before she had finally shouted out, "We can't keep doing this! He's going to hear us and it'll be devastating." It was too late. Thomas had already heard it. Now he was in his bed at *H.E.A.R.T.* recalling the conversation from years earlier. The tremendous guilt that Thomas had felt back then started to resurface. Anger. Frustration. Resentment. He wasn't sure what he was feeling... because it felt like all of them.

Thomas had been at *H.E.A.R.T.* for a while before Kenny had arrived. They never spent much time together and rarely engaged in conversation. Thomas always had friends that he trusted, but things had begun to change as Kenny's evening sessions had grown. Not everyone felt the same level of excitement and appreciation about Kenny's stories, and Thomas was one of them. He wasn't sure what bothered him more: the content of Kenny's stories or the fact that the different patients who had previously eaten lunch and spent time with Thomas were now congregating near Kenny.

Thomas found himself socializing with those patients less frequently. He also didn't get many visitors, which only increased his feelings of isolation from everyone else. Meanwhile, as Kenny's popularity with the other patients continued to grow, Thomas felt even more isolated and resentful towards Kenny. He had begun talking to other patients who had not been going to Kenny's story telling time and started to share negative things about him.

Eventually, the division between the two groups had widened. They no longer wanted to do any activities together, and it became known as "Kenny's group" and "Thomas's group". Frustrated that "Kenny's group" kept slowly growing in numbers, Thomas had tried to convince his group that they should tell their parents that Kenny was making up stories that could be harmful to the other patients. Although they did not want to upset Thomas, the other members of his group were reluctant to go to the doctors, or to their parents, because they could not pinpoint any specific negative behavior coming from Kenny.

Thomas was having a lot of trouble believing the information Kenny was sharing with the other patients because he could only accept beliefs that were in line with how he felt inside. Compounding his struggles, his parents were coming to visit today and he could feel the resentment that his father had towards him. He believed it was all his fault that his parents weren't able to do a lot of the things they had always dreamed they would. Unknowingly, deep inside he was feeling similar resentment towards Kenny.

He would at least have a lot more friends at *H.E.A.R.T.* if not for Kenny. His frustration was hitting a boiling point. He wondered how Kenny could be allowed to keep this group of friends going. His frustration slowly turned to anger. His mind kept wandering… thinking about what he could do. He kept coming back to the same thought: *I can't change how my parents treat me, but I may be able to change how other patients treat Kenny.*

When Thomas's parents arrived at *H.E.A.R.T.*, they met in one of the conference rooms with his primary physician. Dr. Gupta was a slight man with a warm smile and a calm disposition. The main purpose of the meeting was to give Thomas's family an update on his condition. The update was not what they had been expecting. The doctor told his parents that unfortunately Thomas's condition was getting worse. The medication treatments were not having the desired effects they had hoped for. The doctors were confused as to why they were recording signs of increased stress levels in his body. His cortisol readings were rising when they should have been coming down based on the medication he was on and as a result… his tumor was no longer shrinking.

His parents were alarmed. "Why do you think this is happening?" his mother asked with rising concern in her voice. "What do you think it could be?"

"We're not sure. We'll have to run more tests," the doctor responded.

*"I know what it is!"* Thomas blurted out.

The doctor and his parents both turned to him in equal astonishment.

"Well, what is it?" his father asked.

Thomas folded his arms defiantly across his chest. "It's all because of Kenny!"

"Kenny?" said his mother. She looked at the doctor and asked, "What is he talking about?"

"Kenny is one of our other patients who has been sharing some non-conventional concepts with a number of the teens," the doctor replied.

"What kind of concepts?" she asked with a growing sense of urgency.

Thomas wasn't going to wait for a response from the doctor. "He said I have two brains and three eyes and that one of my brains would heal me. That's why I stopped taking my medication!"

Thomas's parents' gasp of disbelief was in unison with the Dr. Gupta's. Just by their reaction, Thomas knew he had created the potential firestorm that would get Kenny's group shut down. His immediate rush of adrenaline was quickly offset by his internal acknowledgment that everything he had just told his parents and the doctor was not true.

"Who is this Kenny character?" his mother demanded. "We have to get to the bottom of this right now!"

Dr. Gupta assured his parents that they would take immediate action to address this situation. He re-convened a meeting of top officials at *H.E.A.R.T.* the very next day and they discussed some of the immediate measures they could take to address Thomas's allegations. While Kenny had many supporters among the staff, the overall consensus was that some form of action must be taken. This included the strict monitoring of all medications by the medical staff, and a letter of caution to Kenny and his parents, demanding an apology by Kenny to Thomas and his family. By the time the meeting was adjourned, they realized the measures they planned to implement would not be enough.

Thomas's parents did not wait for *H.E.A.R.T.*'s response to what they perceived as Kenny's reckless behavior. They decided to take matters into their own hands and get public opinion on their side. Thomas's mother had created an online blog where she had been sharing the continued progress of her son's medical journey. It had gained a significant following because she consistently referenced other blogs and chat rooms that focused on critical illnesses.

That same day, she blasted *H.E.A.R.T.* in her blog, and Kenny in particular, and said it was an outrage that one of the patients was allowed to deliberately spread lies and a false sense of hope to the other patients. She shared what Thomas had revealed to them and how the hospital's willingness to let Kenny spread false information to the other patients had had a significantly negative impact on her own son's health. Not realizing that the misinformation was coming from Thomas and not from Kenny, readers were infuriated. The news that a hospital designed to treat critical illnesses was endangering the health of its patients went viral. It wasn't long before local television stations got word of the drama and started reporting on the situation. Television and radio crews lined up outside of *H.E.A.R.T.* The senior staff were inundated with requests for interviews and explanations.

Once Thomas's parents left, he went into the Community Room and found Stevie looking out at all the commotion outside the main window.

"What's going on out there?" she asked Thomas.

Thomas turned to her and said, "Don't worry. Kenny's toast."

"Why is that?" Stevie replied with a puzzled tone.

"I told the doctors and my parents that he wanted all of us to stop taking our medication."

"But he never said that. He said we all have the ability to make healthy proteins in our bodies, and if we learned to do this really well, eventually we wouldn't need medication."

"Who cares?" said Thomas coldly. "It's the same thing. He had to be stopped. Kenny the Whiteboard Guy is going down."

"For trying to help us? No, Thomas, it's you who has to be stopped." Stevie stood up and left Thomas alone in the room.

⚜ ⚜ ⚜

Inside the *H.E.A.R.T.* facility, the patients and staff tried to maintain some sense of normalcy while the media frenzy was going on outside. It was not easy to do. Parents immediately flocked to the hospital to talk with their children and see if they had been negatively affected by the insane ramblings of one of the other patients. Before the new hospital measures had even been implemented, most of Kenny's evening group members had been forbidden to associate with Kenny anymore.

H.E.A.R.T.'s senior staff had had enough of Kenny's teachings as well. The repercussions of his misguided views were swift and extensive. All procedures for the administering of medications were reviewed by medical staff. Kenny's evening sessions were immediately prohibited and a strict curfew was instituted for their entire floor. Kenny's parents were summoned to H.E.A.R.T. and they were quickly seated with H.E.A.R.T.'s Chief of Staff.

"As you could surmise from the media," Dr. Lee began. "Kenny has been spreading 'tall tales, if you will, to all of the other patients and it has started to have a negative effect on their progress."

"What kind of stuff is he saying to them?" asked his father.

"He's telling them that they have two brains…and that one of the brains can cure their illnesses, so they don't need to take their medications."

"Where is he getting those ideas?" his mother interjected. "Is someone feeding him that nonsense?"

"We're not really sure. We were hoping you could help us with that."

His mother was taken back. "Us? Why do you think we would know anything about it?"

"He's not getting those stories from you?"

"Are you kidding? Of course not!" exclaimed his father.

"Well, I can assure you," said the Chief, "we will get to the bottom of this."

It didn't take much time before other parents started to debate this on social media. As it went viral with many different versions of the truth, the local press got more involved. Soon there were protesters at the hospital and they wanted to know why the hospital allowed Kenny to talk about made up tales. They started to call it a cult.

Rumors continued to spread throughout the hospital and patients moved back over to Thomas's group in droves. They made fun of Kenny and he felt embarrassed. He immediately stopped talking about Carlos. It wasn't long before he began to question whether Carlos had ever existed.

Meanwhile, Kenny's parents tried to make sense of it all.

"We just want to know where all this came from," they pleaded with him.

"I just made it up, okay?" he said defiantly. "I'm sorry. I don't know what I was thinking."

"That's not good enough," his father shot back. "Do you know how many people you hurt by telling all these stories?"

"I don't know what you want me to say. I already said I'm sorry."

"How do we know it's not going to happen again?" his mother asked.

"You don't have to worry about that anymore. I'm done making up stories." The tone in his voice was convincing enough for his parents.

As a result of all of the negative media coverage, *H.E.A.R.T.* issued a public apology for allowing nonmedical propaganda to be disseminated to parts of the hospital. The apology was received with mixed reviews. The senior staff realized they had a serious public relations issue to contend with. They had to reinforce the values and culture that they had always maintained. A new public relations firm was hired to survey the damage and make recommendations going forward. Changes were inevitable.

# Chapter 11
## Enter Dr. Jon

Kenny was struggling. He was not only mad, but he was losing faith. He blamed Thomas for the backlash he'd created and for making Kenny feel so miserable. He started to feel that the cancer was in control again, and his health took a turn for the worse. He stopped talking to the other patients and the isolation he felt was reminiscent of his time before *H.E.A.R.T.* Without even Carlos to talk to, he had never felt so lonely in his life.

As days passed, he kept reliving the same episode with Thomas over and over. Each time, he felt the same feelings of confusion and shame. He stopped paying attention to everything else going on around him and was confined to his bed all day long. It wasn't really a choice. He couldn't muster the strength to get up. His medical treatments felt more debilitating on his body than ever before and the days all started to blur together. When he opened his eyes one afternoon, he saw an imposing figure with jet black hair looking down at him. He smiled at his father.

Matt Haneg usually stayed in the background. His wife was intensely involved in every aspect of Kenny's treatments so it appeared that he was out of the picture for much of the time. But he was always there. If not in person, he was there in spirit. On this day, he was standing in front of Kenny.

"Hi, Dad," Kenny mustered in a soft tone.

"Hi, Kenny. Are you feeling any better?"

"Not really."

"I'm sorry to hear that, son."

"Where's mom?"

"Your mother will be back to see you very soon."

"That's good."

"She's really looking forward to seeing you," his father replied with an unexpected level of excitement.

Kenny noticed the change in his father's tone. "Is everything okay?"

"Everything is better than okay," his father responded.

"Can you share anything?" Kenny pleaded. "I could really use some good news right now."

"We were going to surprise you…but your mother had the baby! You are now officially a big brother."

Kenny let out a scream of joy that doubled as an explosion of pent-up emotions.

Finally, there was something to be happy about. Over the next few days, somehow the treatments seemed a little more manageable. As soon as it was possible, his parents brought his baby sister to see him and he was overjoyed with the sight of this beautiful little creation. As he was lying in bed thinking of his new-born sister, he remembered sharing the initial news of his mother's pregnancy with Carlos.

"So now my baby sister is born," he whispered, not expecting a reply. "I guess you know that already."

"Yes, I do," responded Carlos as he tried to control his excitement of communicating with Kenny again.

"Of course. *Now* you're here. You always show up for the good times. Where did you go? You disappeared and left me all alone."

"I never went anywhere," Carlos replied.

"Yes, you did. Just when everyone started laughing at me, and I started wondering if you were even real, you never showed up."

"When you started listening to the negative opinion of others, and to doubt me, that's when you stopped being able to communicate with me."

"But you're here now," Kenny replied flatly.

"Once again, it was your baby sister. You raised your vibrations up to meet me because of the joy you felt inside when you heard she was born. As I have said, I am always here. But you need to feel good in order to feel me, because I am not going to start feeling bad just so I can go down to your level."

"How can I feel good when other patients are laughing at me?" Kenny asked.

"You never have to let other people dictate how you feel. You can always control how you feel but you give that power away to them."

"Here we go again," said Kenny with a rising level of frustration. "It always comes back to me. I know, it's all my fault. Let's just be real, okay?"

"Okay."

There was a pause. Kenny realized that Carlos was waiting for him to finish his thought.

"It was great while it lasted, but now I have to face reality," Kenny continued. "I'm really sick and I don't have much time left."

"If that is how you are feeling again, then that is what we must experience."

"Don't worry, Carlos. I'm okay with it. We'll just go back to the *Field*."

"Don't worry, Kenny. I'm okay with it too. I love being in the *Field*."

"Good. Then we're at peace, right?"

"Yes, we are," answered Carlos.

There was another long pause while Kenny absorbed the magnitude of what they were sharing with each other. For the first time, it *really* hit him that his dash was going to end soon.

Carlos broke the silence. "I just have one more question. What happens then?"

"What do you mean?" asked Kenny.

"What happens when we're back in the *Field*... watching all the *Lands*... observing all the human beings experience themselves?"

"We just enjoy it, I guess."

"We will enjoy it," agreed Carlos. "But then what?"

There was another pause.

"We start thinking about this human experience we had?"

"Exactly. And then what?"

"We think about what we could have done differently?"

"Exactly. And then what?" Carlos repeated.

Kenny thought about it, and his eyes widened. "We'll want to go back into the Lottery to do it again?"

"Exactly."

"Wow! I didn't think about that. I don't need to go back into the Lottery. I'm already here."

"Exactly."

"Then what do we do now?" asked Kenny.

"We be whoever we want to be, and then we experience whatever we want to experience. Do you remember your free will?"

"Yes. You said it was to be you or not to be you."

"Who are you being right now?" Carlos asked.

"I was me … all alone. But now I'm joined with you."

"What does that mean to you?" asked Carlos.

"Well, 'I am' is my awareness of being."

"Very good. And who am I?"

"My eternal being," Kenny responded confidently.

"So … to be me is to …?"

"… be my eternal being," Kenny finished. "'I am you' means that I'm aware of being my eternal being."

Instantly, Kenny felt a bolt of light shine through his forehead. He could feel every cell in his body dance within him. He was fully aware of being an eternal being in physical form. The density of his body was being lifted. He was Carlos and Carlos was he. This was what he'd come to Gaia for. The realization of being Carlos overwhelmed him.

"I don't want to go back yet," said Kenny. "I just want to be aware of being an eternal being in this human body. This feels amazing."

"You will get no resistance from me," said Carlos. "The *Field* is simply reflecting back to you your awareness of being me. As always, we get to experience this together."

"Yes, and now I understand what you meant when you said that 'our communion is our union'."

⚜  ⚜  ⚜

Gradually, Kenny started to return to the Community Room. He was careful not to mention his renewed conversations with Carlos, but he was able to participate in some group activities. His favorite was movie night because the lights went out and he could absorb himself in the movie without anyone staring at him. As he walked into the room one movie night, he looked around to find himself a comfortable seat. The brightly-colored couches were arranged in a semi-circle to allow for better viewing of the movie. Kenny sat on the end of one of the couches in the third row where he could keep to himself. As the movie progressed, his mind started to wander and his spirits picked up although he couldn't identify why. When it was finished, he stayed seated as all the other patients were helped back to their rooms. After a few more minutes, his imagination was running wild and he couldn't wait to share his thoughts with Carlos.

"We watched *Aladdin* tonight," he said after returning to his room.

"Yes, I know."

"I wish I had a magic lamp too."

"What would you wish for if you had a magic lamp?" asked Carlos.

"That's a silly question. I would wish to be better."

"And why do you need a magic lamp to wish that you were better?"

"Because the genie inside would be able to grant my wish."

"What do you think the genie is?"

"Someone who can make wishes come true," Kenny said.

"What do you think I am?" Carlos asked.

"Well, you're my friend that nobody else can see."

"In other words, I am your non-physical friend?"

"Yeah."

"Would you say that the genie is Aladdin's non-physical friend?"

Kenny considered this. "Yes, I guess you could say that. But you're a part of me."

Carlos continued. "Why do you think that the genie is not a part of Aladdin?"

"Because he came out of the bottle to help Aladdin."

"Where did I come from?"

Kenny paused. "I don't know. You just appeared."

"I am part of your consciousness, Kenny, just as the genie is part of Aladdin's consciousness. Aladdin makes a wish and truly believes that the genie can grant the wish."

"Yeah, so?"

"If you make a wish to me and truly believe that I can grant the wish, you will start to feel as if the wish is already granted. That feeling is what determines whether or not your wish comes true."

"Are you saying that if Aladdin didn't believe the genie could grant a wish, then it wouldn't come true?" Kenny questioned.

"That is exactly what I'm saying. The genie has become the non-physical part of Aladdin and he must believe that the genie has the power to make his wish come true. Likewise, I am the non-physical part of you. When you make a wish, I have already granted it. But it is up to you whether or not you experience it."

"So, it's up to me again?"

"It's always up to you," Carlos responded.

"Why?" Kenny shouted. After a brief pause, his shoulders slumped and he fell back into his black chair. He collected his thoughts before continuing. "Carlos, I'm so tired and I just want to be better. I don't want to have to do anything to get better. The genie could just snap his fingers and I'd be well. Can't you do that for me?"

"But that is acknowledging that you are not well now. And if your belief is that you are not well, then you can't be well."

"But that's the truth! I am not well now."

Carlos corrected him. "That is your perception of the truth."

"No, that is the truth."

"Am I a part of you?" asked Carlos.

"What? Well, yes, I'm talking to you now...and I'm talking to myself...so I guess you're a part of me."

"Am I 'well' right now?"

Kenny shrugged. "I guess so. But once again...you're not real."

"I am not physical, but that does not mean I'm not real. I am vibrational, and everything in your physical universe is vibrational too. Once you realize that you are vibrationally well, you will understand how you can be physically well too. You just haven't seen it yet."

Kenny frowned. "How can I be physically well if I can't see it physically?"

"Let's go back to a previous analogy. If you plant a tomato seed, do you know that seed will become a tomato as long as you keep watering it?"

"Yes."

"Can you see the physical tomato when you plant the seed?"

"No."

"Do you know it's there, even though you can't see it?"

Kenny shrugged. "I guess so."

"It's the same with your desires. If you know you are one with me, then think of me like a seed. You state your intention, or your desire, and I become it, even if you can't see it yet. Then, as long as you maintain your connection with me, which is like watering your plant, you know you will eventually be able to see that intention in your physical world."

"Okay, if my wishes are like seeds...how many seeds do I get?"

"I am all your seeds. You can plant as many desires as you can dream of. So, it's not the seed that matters for you. It only matters that you water the plant. Feeling appreciation for what is to come is the secret to manifesting your desires. You feel the joy of imagining that you already have achieved a desire, and you hold onto that feeling until it manifests. Then you get to enjoy the feeling of achieving it again when it does manifest in your physical world."

"That sounds good. But I make a lot of wishes and you don't grant all of them."

"Kenny, I listen to all your wishes and I grant them all. But your wishes don't come from your words. They come from your thoughts, and your feelings about those thoughts. As long as you feel the joy of your thoughts coming true, you make it so easy for me to deliver them. Be happy and focus on what you want. Then we are in alignment. Then I will deliver your wish. But as soon as you feel as if your wish won't come true, then you've tied my hands. It's like you've changed wishes. Your new wish is that you don't want it to come true. I must deliver your new wish, which is that you can't have what you want. You see, it is not that I don't deliver all your wishes. I always deliver all your wishes. It's just that you change your own wishes by how you feel about those very wishes you wish to create."

"Really?" said Kenny. "You're always granting my wishes?"

"Yes. I am granting all of your wishes every day."

"And what if I don't make any wishes that day?"

"Then I am granting the ones you made yesterday...and the day before."

"But I don't remember those wishes," said Kenny.

"I do. Those wishes are all the thoughts and feelings and beliefs about yourself that you have stored away. Any day that you don't make new wishes or give me new instructions, I keep granting the old ones. Or in other words, I keep running the old programs."

"But I may not want to experience those wishes anymore."

"Then change them."

"Why don't *you* change them!" Kenny implored. "You know what I like. You know what my desires are. You know what's good for me. We're one...remember?"

"I can't," said Carlos.

"What do you mean you can't? You just told me you can grant me any wish I desire."

"That's right. I can grant any of your wishes. But just like the genie in the bottle, no matter how powerful I am, I do not make the wishes. I only grant them. Your wishes are the combination of your thoughts and emotions. They are not only your desires; they are your beliefs ... or what you feel to be true."

"This is crazy!" Kenny exclaimed. "You have all this power. Can't I just instruct you to take care of me?"

"*You* take care of you," said Carlos. "Don't you understand? You keep saying that I have all the power, but if I just have the power to grant your wishes, then you are really the one with all the power – because you determine which wishes are granted."

"*I* have all the power?" Kenny asked incredulously. "Now you're being ridiculous."

"Is that so?" answered Carlos. "Let me ask you a question: who is more powerful, Aladdin or the Genie?"

"That's a silly question. The genie is much more powerful."

"Let me ask you a different question. Who makes the wishes, Aladdin or the Genie?"

"Aladdin."

"Does the genie ever grant his own wishes?"

Kenny paused. "I don't think so."

"That's right. So, if the Genie only grants the wishes of Aladdin, and Aladdin determines which wishes he wants granted, who is more powerful ... Aladdin or the Genie? Or better yet, who gets all their wishes granted ... Aladdin or the Genie?"

"Aladdin?" Kenny guessed.

"Correct. If Aladdin never makes a wish, does the Genie grant his wish?"

"Well ... I guess not."

"Is the Genie still with him?"

"I guess so."

"He is," said Carlos. "The genie is right there ready to grant Aladdin's wish, but he never gets to use his powers because he needs to wait for Aladdin to activate his powers. Aladdin must identify his desires and then clearly express his wishes to the Genie. True?"

"Yes. That's true."

"Well," said Carlos, "we have the same relationship."

"How so?"

"I am always with you too. I am here waiting for you to identify your desires and to clearly express your wishes to me. At that point, I don't choose to grant your wishes. I have already become them and they are simply reflected back to you from the *Field*. It is law."

"Like the mirror, right?" asked Kenny.

"Yes. Like the mirror."

⚜ ⚜ ⚜

Kenny started to enjoy his renewed communion with Carlos. He still didn't interact with the other patients very frequently, but when he passed any of his friends in the hallways, he was reassured by a simple nod or smile coming from them. He had never expected to be a teacher. He was always the pupil and now he was relishing that role again.

While the patients at *H.E.A.R.T.* began to return to their normal routine, the same couldn't be said for the hospital staff. The repercussions of the negative media exposure resulting from the feud between Thomas and Kenny would take time to recover from. Although the constant social media storm was subsiding, it continued to re-emerge on a regular basis. The public relations firm hired to address the issue spent several weeks interviewing staff, patients and their parents.

One of their first recommendations was to make a significant new hire to the medical staff, to show that the institution was taking this very seriously. The intention, as explained by the PR firm, was that in order for *H.E.A.R.T.* to address all the critics of their perceived shift to non-conventional treatments, they had to better understand what this area of science had discovered. They had done an extensive talent search and come up with a candidate who could address many areas of concern. Most importantly, he was a premier doctor in the area of non-conventional treatment for critical illnesses. His name was Dr. Jon Dellorusso.

Dr. Jon's journey to *H.E.A.R.T.* was not a conventional one. He had wanted to be a doctor since as early as he could remember. He had envisioned himself as a member of the established medical community. That was before his sister had been diagnosed with myasthenia gravis. At the time, he had thoroughly researched her condition and been comfortable with the medications she was prescribed. After the first few years, her prognosis had been expected to improve dramatically. Instead, it had only got worse.

As her condition had deteriorated and the doctors had declared that there was nothing more they could do, Dr. Jon had started exploring alternative forms of treatment involving the power of thoughts and emotions on the expression of genes in the body. His sister had trusted him and they had worked diligently together on new techniques. Slowly, her body had started producing healthy proteins that had eradicated the negative effects of her disease. Her doctors had been unable to explain the positive change in her condition. Dr. Jon knew what it was. From that moment on, he had dedicated his career to exploring alternative forms of treatment for both terminal and non-terminal illnesses. He had never imagined it would lead him to *H.E.A.R.T.*

Dr. Jon was aware of the negative publicity that *H.E.A.R.T.* had endured over the past couple of months and his first order of business was to sit down and talk with Kenny. He found his conversations with Kenny extremely informative. It became obvious to him that Kenny was not the cause of the misinformation that was spreading through social media about *H.E.A.R.T.* It was also apparent to him that Kenny was not getting his information from other people. He was accessing information from a field of energy. It was the same as the quantum field that he had been studying.

Over the course of several conversations with Kenny during his first week at *H.E.A.R.T.*, they discussed many of the concepts that Carlos had shared with Kenny. Those concepts included the *Lens of Love,* Kenny's *Heart Brain* and the activation of his *Third Eye.*

"Science is just starting to explain many of the things that you have already learned from Carlos," said Dr. Jon.

Kenny was not satisfied. "If science and Carlos are saying the same thing, then why do people believe what you say about science and not what I say about Carlos?"

"That is an excellent question. So far, most people have not been able to tap into the information you have received from Carlos. But don't forget, you are not using what you learned from Carlos to try to explain science. You are just trying to align with that consciousness. Science is a method of trying to explain what you already understand. People tend to trust the explanation that science gives, mostly because they can't yet tap into the consciousness that you have tapped into... and they need an excuse as to why not."

"I believe everyone can tap into the consciousness of the *Field,*" Kenny responded firmly.

"That doesn't surprise me," said Dr. Jon. "Belief is a very powerful force within the quantum field. You could even say it is the language of the field." He paused for a moment before going on. "Kenny, you seem to have developed incredibly strong beliefs that are not influenced by outside forces. Can you share more of that with me?"

"It hasn't been easy," said Kenny. "I had many bouts of doubt and frustration before I could see myself as being healthy."

"That's interesting," said Dr. Jon. "Are you saying that you don't identify with the patient I'm looking at right now?"

"Not the sick patient."

"How do you do that?" asked the doctor.

"I don't see that *me* anymore."

Dr. Jon was intrigued. "What *me* do you see?"

"Well, others may look at me and see a sick person in a hospital. I used to see that same sick person as someone that other students were making fun of at school. It just reinforced that image of who they thought I was. Then I started observing that person. I started observing who I *was* versus who I *could be*. Once I did that, I started to realize that who I could be was a different person from who I was. Then I started asking, 'Who else could I be?'"

"Keep going," said Dr. Jon.

"The more I observed myself, I started noticing many different *me's*. There was a *healthy me*, there was a *sick me*, there was a *young me*, there was an *old me*, a *happy me* and an *angry me*. I could see them all existing simultaneously. Carlos helped me figure out how to be the *me* that I wanted to be, and not the *me* that other people thought I was."

"And how do you do that?"

"First, I have to pick the *me* that I want to be," Kenny explained. "I focus on that, and then I imagine how it would feel to be that *me*. That feeling creates the projection of who I am being, and then who I am being creates the reflection of what I experience."

"How do you pick the *me* that you want to experience?" Dr. Jon asked.

"Some of these *me's* I created from past images and experiences. Some I've created from future images … or my imagination. Those are the ones I want to experience going forward."

"Quantum superposition." Dr. Jon said out loud.

"What's that?" asked Kenny.

"It's kind of what you just described."

"I'm not sure I understand."

"In the field of quantum physics, we have discovered that there is an electromagnetic field of energy in which a particle can exist in several different states at once. In other words, it contains all potential possibilities at the same time. The one that you observe, or focus on, becomes the one that converts from energy into matter, or from a wave to a particle."

"That's just like the *Field of Potential Probabilities*!" exclaimed Kenny.

Dr. Jon smiled. "It certainly is."

❖　❖　❖

Kenny was ecstatic that Dr. Jon was reinforcing the messages from Carlos in scientific terms. Later that day, he was alone in his room and got the opportunity to share his excitement with Carlos. After he told Carlos what Dr. Jon had said, he admitted that he was feeling that Dr. Jon had essentially redeemed him.

"Dr. Jon says there is a field that envelops everything, and that we humans can access a higher level of consciousness by accessing this field. Is he talking about the *Field of Potential Probabilities*?"

"What do you think?" asked Carlos.

"I think he is."

"So do I."

"I can't believe it!" exclaimed Kenny.

"What did you think … I was making this all up?"

"Well, everyone else thought I was making it all up. But Dr. Jon doesn't think that. He told me that the cells in my body respond to the environment. He's talking about the *Field* again, right?"

"Yes, he is," Carlos acknowledged. "Your environment is either the frequency of the *Field*, which originates internally, or it is the frequency of the *Land of Perception and Time*, which originates externally. And it is true: your body is always responding to one of them. So, the only question you need to concern yourself with is: Which environment is your body responding to right now?"

❖　❖　❖

As Chief of Staff, Dr. Jin Lee was the highest-ranking member of the staff at *H.E.A.R.T.* and had reluctantly agreed to bring Dr. Jon on board. Dr. Lee had already gone down the path of alternative medicine and was not convinced a second time down that road would be any more successful … but he did not have any better alternatives. Before he'd arrived at *H.E.A.R.T.*, he had been an accomplished acupuncturist who specialized in treating infertility. He had envisioned the hospital embracing his specialty and setting up a whole new unit at *H.E.A.R.T.* to focus on acupuncture and related practices for post-natal care of critically ill patients. He had never been given the chance.

"We appreciate your enthusiasm for your vision," he'd been told. "But right now, our immediate need is to raise enough funds for the new equipment we have already identified as crucial to our success going forward."

Dr. Lee had taken this as a challenge and discovered that he was a prolific fundraiser. He'd organized a group called *The Friends of H.E.A.R.T.* and they had raised several million dollars for the purchase of the new medical equipment. He had been praised for his work within the hospital and the community. He'd then quickly expanded his fundraising efforts which enabled them to bring in some of the most advanced technology in the country, including those related to artificial intelligence and brain-computer interfaces. His vision of the future had shifted to the continued development of technology and he had been rewarded with a promotion to *H.E.A.R.T.*'s Chief of Staff. He was not going to allow Dr. Jon to take them backwards.

Meanwhile, Dr. Jon continued speaking with Kenny and many of the other patients on Kenny and Thomas's floor. He documented these discussions while he formulated the recommendations he would be making. It was soon time for him to share his initial findings with senior members of the hospital staff.

Dr. Jon surveyed the boardroom through his dark-rimmed glasses as he sat at the far end of the large mahogany desk. He wore a tailer-made suit that highlighted the athletic frame he developed through years of exercise and healthy eating habits. The room was smaller than the auditorium and it filled up quickly as the doctors were curious as to what information Dr. Jon had come up with. A buzz of chatter and a feeling of anticipation permeated the room. Once everyone had settled down, Dr. Jon addressed the staff:

"I want to start by letting you know what the new sciences are teaching us. The most relevant point is that our thoughts and emotions do have a significant effect on the cells of our body. They don't make genetic changes in our DNA, but they can change how our bodies read the DNA sequence. So, there is actually a lot of truth to what Kenny has been saying to the other patients."

The room immediately erupted into separate conversations overlaid with skepticism.

"Calm down, everyone," Dr. Jon pleaded. "The latest science tells us that our cells *are* affected by their environment."

Dr. Lee was open to new ideas but he was not ready to accept what Kenny was saying as true. "Dr. Jon, I understand that the cells in our body react to our external environment. That's why we are already giving our patients the best possible environment here at *H.E.A.R.T.*"

"The cells in our body don't only react to what is happening in our external environment," responded Dr. Jon. "That's a myth. They also react to our *perception* of what's happening in our environment. The cells in our body are signaled based on our interpretation of the information we receive about both our external and internal environment. Kenny is giving some of the patients a new interpretation of everything their environment is throwing at them by changing how they think and feel. It's a new interpretation of everything that we are giving them ... and I can't say he is wrong."

"Are you implying that how our patients think and feel can actually heal them?" said Dr. Lee incredulously.

"I am not implying it. I'm stating it as a fact."

"There is no definite proof that any of this is true!" shouted one of the doctors. "He's talking about changing his biology. We don't even know if this is possible."

Dr. Jon ignored the renewed commotion coming from the audience and continued to speak over the staff.

"We have trillions of cells in our body, and we're constantly producing more cells at every moment. We're capable of producing healthy cells no matter what's going on in our external environment. You all know about the placebo effect. Just contemplate that for a minute. Really ask yourself how it's possible that countless studies show virtually no statistical difference in a patient's recovery from prescribed medication versus taking a bunch of sugar pills. If someone believes they are going to get better because they believe they are taking medication to cure them, and they get better even though they only took a sugar pill, the only logical conclusion is that it was their 'belief' in getting cured that actually did cure them. Your belief comes from your thoughts and emotions. That is what Kenny is telling them."

Dr. Lee was not convinced. "That's not what he is telling them. He's telling them wild fantasy stories."

"Then let me ask you a question," Dr. Jon countered. "What is the difference between someone who gets cured because they took a sugar pill, and someone who gets cured because their eternal being wrote a new script for the movie of their life that helped cure them? In both cases, their newfound health came from the belief that they were becoming healthy."

Another burst of clatter erupted from the room.

"You can't link what he's saying back to the placebo effect!" shouted one doctor.

"Why not?" asked Dr. Jon in a calm voice.

"Because you have no data to back it up!" he replied.

"Actually, I do," said Dr. Jon.

The room quieted down immediately. "What kind of data?"

"After talking to Kenny, I started to look at all the remission rates at the hospital over the past two years. I noticed a slight overall improvement in total remission rates during the time of Kenny's night-time talks."

"That's my point!" the doctor interjected. "A slight overall improvement doesn't validate what he was teaching."

"That's true," Dr. Jon continued. "That's why I dug a little deeper. I divided the patients into two sample groups. One was labeled 'K' for Kenny and the other was labeled 'T' for Thomas. As you know, Thomas is one of our patients who has led a group that has strongly opposed Kenny's views. It turns out that not only were all the improvements shown in 'Group K' but all the decreases in progress were made in 'Group T.'

The buzz in the room started to pick up again to a feverish pitch.

"Ladies and gentlemen, please!" Dr. Jon called out. "These are the facts. I will be publishing the results in the hospital's medical journal and I'll let you all examine them for yourselves. At that time, I would like to request that we reconvene and discuss this topic further."

"And what do you suggest we convey to our patients and their parents in the meantime?" asked Dr. Lee.

"I guess my message to them would be…if you can think thoughts of being sick, or you can think thoughts of already being healthy, I would spend all my time thinking thoughts about being healthy. Now, that doesn't mean we'll stop treating you. We will continue to do everything we can to keep trying to get you better. But it's like trying to save someone from drowning. If they keep kicking and fighting while you're trying to bring them to shore, they make it much harder for you to save them. If they relax and just kick their feet a little, they make it much easier for you to save them."

"This isn't over," said Dr. Lee. He adjourned the meeting for one week.

⚜ ⚜ ⚜

After the staff meeting, Dr. Jon set up individual consultations with a number of the patients' parents. The first one would be the most challenging. It was with Thomas and his parents. He began by explaining to his parents that Thomas's condition was predicated on what he believed to be true and not what Kenny was telling him.

"But Kenny was telling him lies," said his mother.

Dr. Jon turned his focus to Thomas. "Thomas, do you believe what Kenny was saying?" he asked.

"No. Of course not," said Thomas.

"So, you don't believe your thoughts and emotions can have a positive impact on your health?"

There was a pause. "No," he said hesitantly.

"Then you're not benefitting from what Kenny was saying. But you weren't being harmed by it either."

"Yes, he was!" his mother shouted.

"How so?" asked Dr. Jon very calmly.

"The things he said were making Thomas very angry… and that can't be good for him."

"No, it can't," Dr. Jon agreed. "But what if some of the things he was saying were actually true?"

"Are you kidding? He was telling them they have two brains!" retorted his mother.

"Thomas, where did he say your second brain is?"

"I don't know. I think he said it's in our heart," Thomas replied in a soft whisper.

"It is."

"It is what?" asked his mother.

"It is in our heart," Dr. Jon clarified.

"What the hell are you talking about?" demanded his father.

"The latest scientific evidence is telling us that the complex nervous system in our hearts has a detailed network of neurons and neuron transmitters, just like our brains. But the brain cells in our hearts are even more powerful than the neurons in the brain that's in your head. We call it your Heart Brain. So yes, he is correct; we all have two brains."

That last statement was too much for his father to accept. "This is ridiculous," he shouted out.

Dr. Jon remained calm. "Whether you feel it is ridiculous or not, what Kenny was telling these patients is not lies. It is not fiction."

"It is to me," said his father as he stood up and walked out of the meeting.

Thomas sat alone in his room contemplating the discussion with Dr. Jon and his parents. It had not gone how he had expected. He had never entertained the possibility that what Kenny was saying could be true. He thought about the disappointment on his dad's face as he'd stormed out of the meeting. Once again, Thomas felt it was all his fault. He felt shame. Suddenly, he was startled by the sound of footsteps and looked up to see his mother standing in front of him.

"Mom, what are you doing here? I thought you and Dad left already."

"Your father is waiting in the car. We need to talk, Thomas."

"What's wrong?" he asked.

"I haven't been completely honest with you."

"About what?"

"You are not the cause of your father's anger, Thomas. He was angry long before you were born. I'm just sorry I let it affect you so much."

"I don't understand."

She proceeded to tell Thomas about the history of her relationship with his father. He had always been prone to anger and she never knew what the root cause of it was. She only knew that he went from blaming her parents to blaming Thomas.

"It's not your fault," she told him. "It's mine. I never stepped in to protect my parents. I won't make the same mistake with you," she promised. "I love you too much."

Thomas didn't know how to respond. Too many thoughts were swirling through his mind. But he was able to pinpoint the one overwhelming feeling that he had. It was a feeling of relief.

⚜   ⚜   ⚜

Dr. Jon did not feel that he'd expressed his findings in the most effective way during the first staff meeting. There was still much skepticism from the staff and word of the meeting had spread throughout the hospital like wildfire. The following week, the attendance at the expanded staff meeting doubled from the previous week, so they needed to move it into the auditorium. There were very few empty seats to be found.

Dr. Jon addressed the audience again. "Most patients, when told they have a critical illness, start to feel greater and greater levels of fear and stress. The more stress they feel, the more fearful thoughts they think. It's a vicious cycle we try to eliminate with medication and drugs. But there is another way. Kenny is teaching them to make their own healing drugs."

"And how are they expected to do that?" asked one of the doctors.

"The new science has proven that the cells in our bodies react to their environment. Kenny intuitively knows that he can't stop his cells from reacting to the environment, but he realizes he can change his environment – not where he is on the outside but where he is on the inside. So he is teaching them to shift their awareness from their external environment to their internal environment. Since cells react to their environment, he is teaching them to love ... so love becomes their environment."

"How can love become their environment?" asked the same doctor.

"Kenny is teaching them to love themselves. They have been programmed to believe that there is something wrong with them. They question why they are here instead of other children. Many of them think they must have done something wrong. He is teaching them that they did nothing wrong. They are perfect just the way they are, and they can love themselves unconditionally. And when they do love themselves unconditionally, *that* is the environment they are creating in their body. *That* is the environment that every cell in their body gets to experience ... and their cells react to that environment in a positive way!"

"But they need to maintain that environment," said another doctor.

"He does. Do you know what he said to me?" asked Dr. Jon.

The doctor shook her head.

"He said, 'I came here to be aware of my breath and to feel only love. Everything else will take care of itself.'"

"I'm sure that helps him, in his own way," responded the doctor.

"Not in his own way," said Dr. Jon. "In every way! In all of our studies, if we can get patients to be consciously aware of their breath and to tap into the elevated emotion of love, they start to change the physiology of their body. Kenny is doing it on his own."

Dr. Jon could feel himself getting too excited, so he paused before continuing. "We know our minds can heal our bodies. We've proven it with teams of doctors, and he has figured out how."

"So, what does that have to do with the stories he's telling these patients? He makes it all seem like a game," shouted another doctor.

"Like playing 'Be Carlos for a Day'?" asked Dr. Jon.

"Yes! He's giving them a false sense of hope."

"He's helping them reprogram their subconscious mind to be healthy instead of being sick," Dr. Jon corrected.

"Oh, come on!" said the doctor skeptically.

"Why do you think he has them play games all the time? Practice is repetition. Repetition forms habits. Habits are like your own personal programs. Your subconscious mind runs on programs. When you're not using your conscious mind, which is 95% of the time, the subconscious mind runs on the programs you have created. We, as a profession, have put very little effort into trying to change their subconscious programs. We give them all kinds of treatments and hope they will get better. Kenny is training them to believe they are already healthy. Belief is more powerful than hope."

"We have had a significant amount of success in this hospital treating critically ill patients," said Dr. Lee, "and it's not just based on hope. It's based on sound medical principles and industry-leading technology. Don't forget…we also have our reputations to uphold."

"That's right," confirmed Dr. Jon. "Our reputations are on the line here. We have always taken all the credit for getting our patients well. We tell them what's wrong with them and we say there's nothing they can do about it. Only we can help them, and they must trust us. Well, no disrespect to anyone in this room…but that creates fear in our patients. That creates stress…and stress up-regulates harmful proteins in their bodies. We then have to treat them for the negative conditions that we ourselves helped to perpetuate. Kenny is telling them that they all have a power within them that can heal them. By looking at their lives through a Lens of Love instead of a Lens of Fear, they are mixing the emotion of love with their thoughts. That becomes the environment that they expose to all the cells in their body, and the result is that they are actually strengthening their immune system. We have scientific proof of it."

"He's playing 'God' with their lives, for Christ's sake!" said Dr. Lee emphatically. "I'm not willing to put the lives of my patients in the hands of another young patient who claims he has access to some super power."

Dr. Jon was undeterred. "He is *not* telling them he has some super powers. He's telling them they have access to their own internal energy source. He's helping them to foster a relationship with their own inner power, not his. And now we know, beyond a shadow of a doubt, that accessing higher energy levels can change the gene expression in our bodies. He is accessing the natural pharmacy that we were all born with, by signaling the genes to produce healthy proteins. We even have concrete evidence that people have lengthened their telomeres, which lengthens their lives. How could we possibly discourage that when there is no downside?"

Dr. Lee started to calm down. "What are we supposed to do – stop giving them their treatments and hope this works?"

Dr. Jon shook his head and lowered his voice. "No. Not at all. We can work in *conjunction* with what he's teaching them. Call it a clinical trial. We continue to administer all of the medical treatments that we have available to us and mix them with the natural healing approach that he is expressing. What's the downside to that?"

The attention of the room went back to Dr. Lee. He was silent for a moment before reluctantly saying, "I don't see any downside."

Another doctor spoke up. "I think it's fascinating what Kenny is saying. But where is he getting this information?"

"Energy is frequency and frequencies carry information," said Dr. Jon. "He's tapping into a field of information that we all have access to. Most of us just don't get there."

"You mean like the quantum field?" asked the doctor.

"That is the best way I would describe it. 'Going quantum' is simply accessing a field of energy that stores unlimited information. Kenny says that when he is in communion with his eternal being, they are in union. This is the equivalent of him accessing a unified field of energy that is storing unlimited information. In both cases, you access that field of energy by tuning into its frequency."

Dr. Lee was going to say something else but suddenly stopped. He found himself contemplating the words he had just heard. *What if*, he thought to himself. *What if Kenny is tapping into the healing energy that science is now only beginning to explain?* He was consumed with the thought of *what if* as Dr. Jon continued speaking.

"We also cannot underestimate the power of our imagination," Dr. Jon explained. "Kenny is teaching them that they can create their internal environment with their imagination. So, if they imagine themselves to be healthy, and they surround themselves with the feeling of being healthy, that becomes their environment."

"And their cells react to their environment," said Dr. Lee as he thought about the magnitude of everything he was hearing.

"Precisely," answered Dr. Jon.

"Oh my God," said a doctor from the second row.

Dr. Jon immediately knew that he had gotten his message across to all the doctors in the room. There was nothing else for him to say at this time.

The meeting was adjourned.

# CHAPTER 12
## LIVING THE LAWS

Kenny stared out of the window in his room and examined the giant sycamore tree in the backyard of *H.E.A.R.T.* He thought about the seed that had been planted in the soil many years ago and how it had grown into this beautiful creation. The tree had always been in the seed even when you couldn't yet see it. But it had been planted, and nurtured, and continued to grow into its original essence.

As he contemplated this evolution, he felt a peacefulness overcome him. Then he looked into the upper branches of the tree and noticed a pattern on the tips of the branches. They were all in unison. He realized this was the pattern of the tree. It was a fractal pattern. It simply kept re-creating itself. Like a computer program continuing to run its original code, the pattern of the tree continued to produce the essence of the seed.

Later that night, he described what he had seen in the tree to Carlos.

"Now you are starting to understand that all of the laws are interconnected," said Carlos. "When you combine an understanding mind with an understanding heart, you don't just see things and think about them. You see things and *feel* them. You feel as if you *are* them. That is how you truly understand them. It is law."

"There you go again saying, 'It is law.' When are you going to teach me about these laws?"

"You have already been living the *Laws of the Field*. You understand how they work. Now you can start to teach them."

Kenny frowned. "What are you talking about? I don't know anything about these *Laws of the Field*."

"Of course, you do."

"How about a little help?" Kenny pleaded.

"Okay. Let's start over. Do you remember our discussion about the mirror?"

"Sure."

"Does the mirror always reflect back to you whatever you project out to it?"

"Yes," said Kenny.

"What else did you learn about the mirror?"

"I should practice my awareness of you in the mirror. And I always have a mirror because the *Land of Perception and Time* is within the *Field*... and the *Field* is a mirror."

"Very good," said Carlos. "Anything else?"

"Yes. Everything I project out into the mirror is reflected back to me."

"No exceptions?"

"That's right."

"So that must be a law."

"I guess you could say that," replied Kenny.

"You *can* say that. It is a law. It is the *Law of Reflection*."

"Hmmmm...."

Carlos continued. "Now what have you learned about planting?"

"That I should practice planting my awareness of you in the garden. And I always have a garden, because the *Field* is the garden."

"Anything else?"

"That whatever you plant in the ground, you always reap exactly what you've sowed."

"No exceptions?"

"No exceptions," confirmed Kenny.

"Would you say that this is a law?"

"I would. What do we call this law?"

"We call it the *Law of Reaping.*"

"Well, that makes sense."

"That's not all. What have you learned about computer programs?"

"I know that they will keep repeating themselves while they are running," Kenny responded.

"Anything else?"

"Well, they won't deviate from that program."

"No exceptions," asked Carlos.

"No exceptions."

"What do you think we call this law?"

"The Law of Programs?" Kenny guessed.

"Not quite. It is the *Law of Repetition.*"

"Okay. I get that."

"Let's share one more," said Carlos. "You and your friends like to sit around and listen to radio programs, don't you?"

"Yes... especially Danny."

"Do you have to tune into a certain station or frequency?"

"Yes."

"What if there isn't a radio station around?"

"We may not get very good reception," said Kenny. "But the *Field* is like a radio station. It's always broadcasting all different programs and I'm like a big antenna that can pick up its frequency."

"Can you tune into one frequency and get a reception on a different frequency?" asked Carlos.

"No."

"No exceptions?"

"No exceptions," agreed Kenny.

"Okay. Then it is law."

"And what do we call this law?" Kenny asked, even though he had a feeling what the response would be.

"It is the *Law of Reception.*"

"You were right," said Kenny. "I already knew about all these laws. I just didn't know they were laws."

"Now that you understand the *Laws of the Field*, it's time to start living them."

"I thought I was."

"Not entirely," said Carlos. "To live them, you must apply them to whatever you are being."

"How do I do that?"

"Just take one at a time. What do you want to be, or feel, more than anything else right now?"

Kenny thought about this for a minute. "Love," he responded.

"Perfect. Now just apply 'love' to each of the Laws and see how it makes you feel."

"Okay. Let me try." Kenny sat back and started to think of one law at a time. Then he spoke out loud: "The *Law of Reflection*: I am being LOVE...and that is being reflected back to me from the *Field*." Kenny smiled as he felt an immediate glow emanating from his solar plexus.

"Very good. Now keep going."

"The *Law of Reaping*: I am sowing LOVE and that is what I am reaping from the *Field*." Kenny could feel the love growing inside of him.

Carlos was pleased. "Keep going."

Kenny continued. "The Law of Repetition: I am programmed to receive LOVE...and that is what keeps repeating in my life."

"One more," said Carlos.

"The *Law of Reception*: I am tuning into LOVE...and that is what I am receiving from the *Field*." The frequency of love rippled through his body.

"I couldn't have said it better myself," said Carlos.

"Now I know that I am love," Kenny replied. "Thank you."

Kenny let that sink in over the course of the next two days. He repeated it over and over as he went through his daily routine. He found himself trying to suppress the smile on his face when he noticed other patients were not feeling the same positive energy that he was feeling. At the end of the second day, he sat in his room and summoned up Carlos again.

"I've been thinking about living the *Laws of the Field*. I found it easy to apply 'love' to the laws. But I just think of how hard it might be for someone else to do this."

"Why do you think that?"

"Let's just say that it must be hard for someone who isn't happy to apply the laws to feeling happy."

"That is true," said Carlos. "The laws don't discriminate between how someone feels. They always honor how you are feeling right now."

"Every time I see Thomas, he always seems angry. Does that mean he is replacing love with anger?"

"Give it a try and see if that makes sense."

Kenny gave it a try:

"I am being ANGRY... and that is being reflected back to me from the *Field*." Kenny started to feel energy draining from his body.

"I am planting ANGER and that is what I am reaping from the *Field*." The feeling of anger started to grow within him.

"I am tuning into ANGER... and that is what I am receiving from the *Field*."

Kenny immediately felt his mood change for the worse. "Holy Mackerel!" he shouted. "Thomas isn't a bad person. He just doesn't understand how the laws work."

"That is true," confirmed Carlos. "Once again, the laws don't change you. Only you can change you, and the laws will express who you are being."

"How do the laws relate to time?" asked Kenny. "How long does it take for them to work?"

"You just found out. How long did it take for you to feel them working?"

"It was immediate, I guess," Kenny replied.

"That's right. The laws are all happening simultaneously. Everything is being reflected from what you are projecting into the *Field*. Everything is being reaped from what you have sown. Everything you experience is a result of the program you are running. Everything is being created from the feeling state that you are tuned into. It is all happening now. So whatever you are feeling right now determines what you are experiencing in this moment."

Kenny thought about the different universal laws and how they each worked flawlessly. Then he started to laugh.

"What's so funny," asked Carlos.

"This is all about the *Field*, isn't it?"

"That's right. It's the Field that does everything. I am only showing you how it works."

"So, if I'm being well …."

"That is reflected back to you from the Field," said Carlos.

"… and if I'm *not* being well …."

"That is being reflected back too."

"That means you are really doing nothing at all?" Kenny kidded.

"Very funny," said Carlos. "I guess not. Now that you understand how the *Field* works, you really don't need me anymore."

"That's not true," said Kenny reassuringly. "You taught me how to feel love. I want to share this feeling with you. Isn't that what you wanted when we came here?"

"Yes, it is. Thank you for allowing me to *Be Me.*"

⚜  ⚜  ⚜

Kenny sat in his black chair and observed himself looking out at the tree in the back courtyard. It never failed to bring him peace of mind. He heard a knock on his door and got up to answer it. He found Thomas standing in the doorway wearing a green surgical gown and white slippers.

"Hey," said Thomas.

"Hey," said Kenny, surprised to see him.

"Do you have a minute?" Thomas asked.

"Sure. Come on in," Kenny invited.

Thomas walked in and looked around the room. He pulled over a dark maroon chair with a high back support so he could sit down next to Kenny. They both stared out at the tree for a short while. Finally, Thomas started to speak.

"I just wanted to say that I'm sorry for all the trouble I caused you."

"It's okay," Kenny said. "Believe it or not, it actually helped me."

Thomas was startled by the response. "How could it have helped you?"

Kenny shrugged. "It helped me find clarity that I might not have found if I hadn't been pushed to go searching for more answers. So ironically, maybe I should be thanking you."

They both chuckled.

"I don't know about that. But maybe you can help me," said Thomas.

Kenny hesitated. He took a good look at Thomas and saw sincerity in his eyes. Then he said, "I'd be glad to help you any way I can."

Thomas paused before responding. He had been so sure of what he was going to say, but now different thoughts raced through his mind. He took a few deep breaths while Kenny showed genuine patience.

"I was always so mad that I had to be here," Thomas began. "And you never seemed to feel that way. I want to understand how you did that. I know I have a long way to go. It's just that I always thought you were so kooky, but then Dr. Jon started to validate what you were saying."

Kenny smiled. He didn't know what to expect from Thomas, but now he felt a tremendous amount of relief flow through his body.

"One thing I have learned," Kenny explained, "is that the first step to changing your life is to want to better understand why you are the way you are. In that case, you're already closer than you think."

Thomas pondered this. "So maybe you and I could start all over?"

"I'd like that," said Kenny.

Thomas and Kenny proceeded to talk all about Thomas's past. Thomas told him how his parents were always at odds with each other and how it always made him feel uncomfortable. Kenny explained how Carlos had come into his life. They shared stories. They laughed together. Before Thomas left, they exchanged contact information and vowed to communicate more often. Thomas gave him a hug as he left the room.

Kenny went back in and sat down on his bed. He thought about the irony of Thomas coming to visit him. His bad behavior wasn't because he was mean – he was just scared.

⚜  ⚜  ⚜

Over the next few months, Kenny focused on living the *Laws of the Field*. Gradually, he started spending more time with his friends again. Dr. Jon published his updated findings from the hospital remission rates and the hospital got rave reviews from the media. Kenny continued to share what he learned about the *Laws of the Field* with Dr. Jon. One morning, Dr. Jon gave him some joyous news.

"Kenny, I don't know how else to say this, so I'll just say it. Your cancer has gone into full remission. We're going to be sending you home to your family completely healthy."

Kenny couldn't move or speak. The joy he was feeling inside was indescribable. His entire stay at *H.E.A.R.T.* flashed before his eyes. Even more clearly, he envisioned the future he was about to experience.

A short while later, he was sitting alone in his room in his favorite black chair.

"Can you believe it!" he exclaimed to Carlos. "I'm finally going home."

"There was never any doubt from me," replied Carlos.

"Guess what else Dr. Jon told me today?"

"What's that?"

"He said that because I was so conscious of you, I affected the nature of reality."

"That is true," replied Carlos.

Kenny stared out at the morning sky as he contemplated what he had just said. "Can I ask you something?" he said sheepishly.

"Of course."

"How did I affect the nature of my reality?"

"As we have discussed many times, the essence of a seed is created by nature and the seed must become the essence of what it is. The essence of a human is created by your intrinsic nature and the human must become the essence of what it is."

Kenny took a moment to collect his thoughts. "So … what is our intrinsic nature … and how can we alter our intrinsic nature … which in effect alters the essence of who we are … and consequently … who we become?"

"Your intrinsic nature is who you are being in any moment. Who you are being is determined by how you are feeling. How you feel is determined by who you imagine yourself to be. Who you imagine yourself to be is called your imagination. Therefore, your imagination is the essence of who you are and that is how you affected the nature of your reality."

"You mean that every time I imagined myself walking out the front door of H.E.A.R.T. completely healed, I was affecting the nature of my reality?"

"That is exactly what I mean," said Carlos.

There were many tearful goodbyes when Kenny left *H.E.A.R.T.* – but they were tears of joy, not sorrow. Kenny expressed his appreciation to all the doctors, nurses and staff who came by to wish him farewell. His friends were all waiting in the Community Room for him and they gave him a giant greeting card to wish him luck going forward. He glanced at all the signatures on the card but his eyes fixated on one signature at the bottom. It was from Thomas.

Kenny's parents were there with his baby sister to take him home. He couldn't wait to spend time with his new sibling. As he walked out the front door of *H.E.A.R.T.*, he suddenly stopped. He was having a flashback. He remembered he had been here before.

But it wasn't a memory from the past. It was once a memory of the future. Only now he was experiencing it in the present.

His parents watched with confusion as he took off his jacket. Underneath, he was wearing the red shirt he'd envisioned a long time ago. He glanced to his left and saw the reflection of himself in a tall mirror. He smiled and Carlos smiled back. The mirror was reflecting back to him the image of who he imagined himself to be. His future memory had become a present reality. A big grin came across his face as he walked through the door for the last time.

"Why did you do that?" his dad asked.

"I remembered this happening – leaving the hospital all cured. I was wearing a red shirt."

"How could you have remembered this? It only just happened."

"I remembered that it had already happened in my imagination," Kenny explained. "It was a future memory." He smiled at his father. "Let's go home, Dad."

**The End.**

Made in the USA
Middletown, DE
25 February 2022

61681311R00102